UNICORNS
IN
THE RAIN

CORNS

IN THE

by Barbara Cohen

Atheneum   New York   1980

RAIN

LIBRARY OF CONGRESS CATALOGING IN PUBLICATION DATA

Cohen, Barbara.
Unicorns in the rain.
SUMMARY: An invitation from a stranger on a train
takes Nikki to unicorns
and the boarding of Noah's ark.
[1. Floods—Fiction] I. Title.
PZ7.C6595Un   [Fic]   79-22082
ISBN 0-689-30735-7

Published simultaneously in Canada by
McClelland & Stewart, Ltd.
Manufactured by R. R. Donnelley & Sons,
Crawfordsville, Indiana
Designed by M. M. Ahern
First Edition

For Rebecca

Imagine a world not in which
God is dead, but to which
He has not yet been born.

UNICORNS
IN
THE RAIN

CHAPTER I

HE WOMAN SHARING MY SEAT WAS very fat. She was so fat that she took up much more than her fair share of space. I was pushed into a corner right next to the train's sooty window. She smelled too, and when she took off her helmet, I could see that her hair was greasy.

I couldn't escape from her. There were no other seats on the train. The aisles were crowded with standees. So I turned my head away and peered out into the deepening twilight. I was in no mood for conversation anyway.

But she was. "Terrible weather, isn't it?" she said, settling her enormous bulk more comfortably and squeezing me yet closer to the window. Half a dozen brightly colored shopping bags pressed against my legs. She really had been all over town. "Rain, or even snow, would be better than this," she continued in a pleasant tone, as if she were talking to

3

my face and not the back of my head.

My sentiments exactly, yet I didn't want to discuss the matter with her. I didn't answer, but pressed my nose against the filthy pane and gazed into the gray twilight.

Once, when I was little, my mother and her boyfriend of the moment had taken me to one of those make-believe old-fashioned villages out in the country. We had wandered in and out of little shops that sold imitation colonial beeswax candles, cobbler bench planters and herb teas, all at inflated prices. I would rather have been at the zoo, where I spent most Sunday afternoons, and I guess I wasn't shy about letting Mother and What's-His-Name know how I felt. To appease me, they took me for a ride on a reconstructed railroad, which ran half-century-old trains from one phony village to another and back again for the benefit of day trippers like us. Whistles, soot, stiff-backed prickly seats and all, that railroad did its job. I was appeased.

So why didn't I find an outing on this bankrupt old railroad equally amusing? What had been fun when I wasn't really going anywhere seemed like a descent into the earth's molten center when I was on an actual journey. Or perhaps I was just too old now to enjoy a train trip for its own sake. I would have been far more contented in an automobile. But my mother had driven the car to the airport, so I was stuck with seats hard as nails, windows so dirty I could scarcely see out of them, and noise so shattering I doubted if my eardrums or intestines would survive the trip. There was something wrong with the power too, and the lights in the car were so dim that it was impossible to read to pass the time. I had investigated other cars when I'd first boarded the train, but they too were filled with the same soiled, choking dimness.

So I sat next to the window and stared out at the damp, dull landscape. It was only a little after four on a mid-November afternoon, but for all that I could see, it might just as well have been midnight. Squares of light from street lamps, windows and automobile headlights shone out through the thick wet mist that lay everywhere. But they illuminated nothing. They merely called attention to themselves. Like the fat lady next to me, I wished it would rain, rain hard. That would be better than the smothering mist that had hung in the air for days. It was so indefinite; it went nowhere, accomplished nothing. Or better yet, let it snow. Let it snow great white flakes that would cover everything with cold restful whiteness, even me. Especially me. But this mist was useless. In it nothing happened. The world outside the train windows was as bleak, as sooty, as airless as the world inside.

I was hot. It was not really cold out, but for some

reason or other, the heat on the train was turned up full blast. I tried to squirm out of my coat, not an easy task with that enormous bulk crowded next to me. My suitcase and her shopping bags on the floor made standing up out of the question. But suddenly I felt her heavy hands grasp my coat collar and my sleeve. She tugged and I wriggled, and a moment later, my coat came off in her grasp. She handed it to me; I folded it and placed it on my lap.

"Thanks," I murmured.

"You're knocked out, dearie," she replied. Her little eyes, partially hidden in folds of flesh, were shrewd. "Take something." She opened her purse, removed a vial of bright green capsules, and pushed it under my nose.

"No thanks." I shook my head.

"Why not?" she asked. "They're good. When I go into a drug shop, I never buy the specials—only name brands. See?" She turned the front of the vial toward me so I could read the label. "High Speed," it said, and then, underneath, "E. L. Kane & Co., Pharmaceuticals." It was one of the best brands, always the same, absolutely reliable.

But I didn't take one. "I've had an upset stomach lately," I said. "I'm trying to lay off for a while."

She nodded. She could accept that. "I'll need every one I have in the house," she said, "just to get through this weekend. Holidays are always awful. Sitting down with a bunch of relatives for dinner once a year is one big pain in the neck."

"I know," I said. "The people I go around with don't bother much with families, not even on holidays."

"You kids have some good ideas," she said. "Why should we celebrate a harvest festival in this day and age, just because some idol-worshipping farmers did it who knows how long ago? It doesn't make any sense."

"It's good for business, they say," I commented. "You have to have holidays."

"Well, let them invent some new holidays, some holidays that'll be suitable for our world. This business of every fool cousin showing up for dinner on a particular day each fall is just plain dumb. Cousins! What'm I bothering with cousins for? Lots of people don't even know who their own father is, and if they do know, they don't care. They're the smart ones."

I had to laugh. "I'm with you," I agreed.

"My kids come, too," she said. "Here I thought once they were out of the house, I'd be rid of them. But they show up every year, like bad pennies, whining and complaining, just the way they did when they were little. Who needs it?" She reached inside her capacious pocketbook again and pulled out a small cellophane bag of salted peanuts. She tore open the bag, leaned her head back, and poured the nuts into her open mouth.

The conductor came through the crowded car, his eyes watchfully darting from side to side. He took his ticket punch out of the same holster in which he carried his gun, punched my ticket and stuck it in the clip on the seat in front of me. But he kept the fat lady's.

"I get off at the next stop," she explained as the conductor moved away. "I hope Arnold's at the station to meet me. I don't relish walking with all these packages. If I needed my gun, I'd never be able to get to it in time."

I bent over to help her organize her belongings. Unaccountably, the side of one of the shopping bags was moving in and out, as if a tiny arm were punching at it from the inside, withdrawing, and then striking out again. I picked the bag up and peered inside.

"Hey, there," the fat lady cried. "What are you doing with my bag? Give it back to me." She began to grope for the pocket of her slacks, no doubt attempting to locate her gun, but her size inhibited her.

Quickly I put the bag back down next to the others. "I'm not trying to steal anything," I hastily assured her. "I just saw the bag move, by itself, and I couldn't help wondering what was in it. You don't

8

have to reach for your gun. I'm not a thief."

"You looked all right," the fat lady said, somewhat mollified. "That's why I sat down next to you. But who can tell, nowadays?"

"Can I look in the bag? Please?"

"Sure. Go ahead." She really was nice enough, at least compared to lots of other people.

I separated the handles of the bag and peered inside. What I saw there was entirely unexpected. A cage of wire mesh enclosed as odd and beautiful a creature as had ever lived. I would have said it was a guinea pig, except that it had long, curly, bright silver hair, randomly streaked with orange. The spaces between the wires were wide enough for it to reach its paw through, and it was clawing away at the side of the bag with a quick, desperate motion. I had a guinea pig at home myself, and it didn't seem to mind its cage, but a cage inside a paper bag was, I supposed, another matter.

"What is it?" I asked.

"A *cavia hirsutus*," the fat lady said. "A longhaired guinea pig. At least that's what they told me in the pet shop."

"You ought to take its cage out of this bag," I said. "It doesn't like being left in the dark."

The woman raised her eyebrows. "Well, isn't that just too bad," she said. "You can just leave that cage where it belongs."

"All right," I said. But then I leaned over and whispered into the bag, "Calm down, honey, calm down. You'll be home soon. Very soon. Very soon, now." I would have liked to reach into the cage and touch the animal, but I was afraid the fat woman would really get mad at me if I did that. Fortunately, the sound of my voice was sufficient. The animal appeared to relax, and the frantic thrusting of its paw against the side of the bag gradually ceased. I turned back to the woman, who was looking at me as if I were crazy. "Why did you buy it?" I asked her.

"For the little boy downstairs," she replied. "My cat ate his other guinea pig."

"What makes you think the cat won't eat this one?"

"Oh, she will, if she gets the chance," the woman replied matter-of-factly. "She's a monstrous cat. Newton just had better be sure to keep the cage locked right and tight this time. Sometimes, though, I think he lets the guinea pig out deliberately. I think he likes to see the cat eat it. It's happened twice already."

I had lied to that guinea pig. I had implied that once it got to the fat lady's house, everything would be all right. "Why did you buy such a fancy guinea pig then?" I asked.

"Oh," she replied airily, "I guess I thought Newton would like something different."

"To say nothing of the cat," I added. She didn't

respond to that remark, but her eyes were shining. She too was looking forward to the battle between the cat and the guinea pig, whether she was willing to say so out loud or not. "Look," I offered, reaching into my purse for my wallet, "how much did you pay for this animal? I . . . well . . . I sort of collect guinea pigs." I was thinking rapidly. "But I don't have one like this. I've never seen one like this. I'd be glad to buy him from you. I'll give you . . . I'll give you half again what you paid for him."

A shrewd glint appeared in her eye. "Twenty-four dollars," she said. "That'd be twenty-four dollars. He cost me sixteen."

An expensive meal for a cat. She was lying, of course. But I didn't argue with her. I pulled out a twenty dollar bill and four singles. That left me with only another single, a five, and some change to last me the whole long weekend. Well, perhaps if I needed money I could borrow some from my grandmother. And I had a couple of credit cards besides.

The fat lady grabbed the money out of my hand and shoved it into her purse. The train creaked painfully to a halt just after that, and she hoisted her enormous quantity of flesh to her feet. As quickly as her bulk would permit, she gathered her packages together and fled down the aisle. She was not going to give me the opportunity to change my mind.

She had kept her part of the bargain, though.

She had left behind the shopping bag with the guinea pig in it. I reached in the bag, lifted out the cage, and put it on my lap. I began stroking the back of the animal's neck with my index finger. "It's all right, honey," I murmured. "It's all right. You're safe now." The guinea pig's eyes shut in total relaxation. He was falling asleep.

In a moment, to my secret surprise, the train managed to cough and sputter and start up again. I hoped that now I would be left alone. I wanted to put my coat and the suitcase jammed between my legs on the seat next to me. But no, a young man was already taking the fat woman's place. I hadn't noticed him before. A few standees remained, although most of them had gotten off or found seats when the train had stopped.

"Do you mind if I sit here?" the young man asked.

I opened my mouth, planning to say, "Would it make any difference if I did?" I looked into his face and changed my mind. What I actually said was, "Sit down, please."

He was the most extraordinarily handsome man I had ever seen. I had the feeling that he had suddenly materialized right next to me, but of course he must have been in the aisle of that very coach all along. How had I missed him? His skin was very dark, and he had huge, heavy-lidded black eyes; a long, thin, straight nose and white teeth that flashed like light when he smiled at me, which is what he was doing that very moment. I could see the thick, shiny black curls that covered his head because, like me, he wasn't wearing a helmet. Some of us had more guts than brains, as the saying goes.

Perhaps not every girl would have thought him so good-looking. Not every woman likes men so dark. But I always had, perhaps because I am so painfully fair myself. I have to sit under an umbrella every second I'm on the beach, and I even have to keep my T-shirt on when I go in the water. I have that freckled white skin that goes with red hair, wildly curly red hair that I can keep in line only by cropping it close. What I wouldn't have given to have been able to wear it long and straight, like Melanie Marsh, who sat next to me in my anthropology class. Well, some people I had known had admired my hair, even if I didn't. Perhaps this sudden masculine presence that had materialized at my side might be among them.

"Thanks," he said. He sat down and tried to find a place for his knapsack where it wouldn't interfere too much with me. Our coach lacked even such a simple amenity as a suitcase rack above the seats. Finally he managed to squeeze it beneath the seat in front of us. "I've never seen this train so crowded," he commented. "Full of lemmings rushing to the sea."

13

Now that I no longer had to stare up at him, he seemed more ordinary, less startling. "Anyway," he continued conversationally, "what is that creature you have on your lap? I don't believe I've ever seen anything quite like it."

"*Cavia hirsutus*," I replied.

Before I could explain, he translated the term for himself. "Hairy guinea pig," he said. "Well, all guinea pigs have a good deal of hair, but this one is ridiculous." He leaned toward me and peered into the cage. "His hair goes down to the floor and curls back up again. How does he manage to get around without tripping?"

"He doesn't have to go far," I said.

"We don't have one like that," he said. "At least I don't think we do."

"What are you?" I asked. "A vet or something?"

"No, no," he replied. "I'm not a vet. My brother is, more or less. I go to law school. Or at least," he added carefully, "I did."

"What's the matter? Are you quitting?"

"I won't be back Monday."

"Why not?"

"It's a long story. Let's just say I'm needed at home."

I was a sophomore at college and had changed my mind about my major five times already. The only reason I stayed was because I wasn't very good at anything else either. But my own lack of purpose didn't stop me from delivering a lecture. "Listen," I said, "that's terrible. I mean, if you managed to get into law school to begin with, it's awful if you can't stay there. Can't you work something out? Borrow money or something?" It was easy to hand out advice I'd find it difficult to follow myself.

"It's not a financial problem," he said slowly. "It's not that at all."

"Whatever it is," I said, "can't they postpone it? Can't it wait awhile?"

He smiled ruefully, a very different smile from the brilliant grin he'd flashed me earlier. "No, it can't wait," he said. "It won't wait."

"Well," I insisted, "I think it's very wrong of your family to make you give up law school. They should know you have a right to your own life."

"It's good of you to be so concerned," he said, "but it doesn't matter. Really, it doesn't matter."

"How can you say that?" I asked him angrily. "How can you say that when it's your life that's being thrown away?" But suddenly I thought of something. "Don't you like law school? Are you doing poorly?"

"Oh, I like it OK, and I'm doing well. I made Law Review." There was a faint note of pardonable pride in his voice.

"Then I can't understand your letting your

family walk all over you," I said. "I can't understand your giving up so easily."

He turned his head and stared at me. "I can't understand your getting so upset over it," he said. "You don't even know me!"

"Well, what's that got to do with it?" I replied testily. "I don't like to see anyone wasting his life."

"Why not?" His voice fell so low that I could hardly hear it above the rattle of the train, and yet it had taken on a curiously insistent quality. "Why not?" he repeated.

"My own life is kind of a mess right now," I said at last. He seemed to be drawing the words out of me. "As a matter of fact, I can't remember when it wasn't a mess. So if you have a direction, or a goal, or something you really like to do, I think you're very lucky, and no one should make you give it up, least of all your family."

"Why is your life a mess?" he asked. "What's wrong with it?"

I echoed his words of a few moments before. "It's a long story."

"Tell me."

"There isn't time." I laughed. "I get off soon—two more stops."

"Why? What's waiting for you there?" he asked, implying by his tone that it couldn't be much. "That town is the pollution center of the universe. You need a gas mask to walk a dog." He looked down at the cage on my lap. "Your poor *cavia hirsutus* won't last a week."

"I won't be there a week," I responded. "My grandmother lives there." I turned my face up to his and looked directly at him. "Can you think of anything more awful than spending a rare, precious holiday weekend with a grandmother you've seen only about twice before in your life?"

"No, I can't think of anything more awful," he agreed, "especially this weekend. So why are you doing it?"

I shrugged. "No choice, really. Mother and her latest are on a plane heading for the tropics right this minute, and the last person Mama wanted on that trip was a sour-faced eighteen-year-old daughter. In fact, that's the very last person she wants anywhere, any time."

"Your face doesn't look sour to me," he said. "If your mother doesn't want you along, I can understand why. It can't be easy to present a boyfriend with a daughter who looks like you."

"Well, thanks," I said. I was startled, but his compliment was delivered so straightforwardly that no other response was possible. "I never looked at it from exactly that point of view before." I wanted to change the subject. "Anyway, she persuaded my father's mother that I ought to spend the weekend with her—get to know each other, she said. It's about time, she said. But if we haven't gotten to know each other in eighteen years, what makes her think we ever want to get to know each other?"

He nodded. "Good point. So, I repeat—why are you going?"

I turned back to my pet and began once again to stroke his fur. "Mother said she couldn't bear the thought of me alone in the apartment while she was off having a good time. The truth of the matter is, she doesn't trust me. She doesn't know who I'd bring into the place, or what kind of wild parties I'd throw." I glanced at him out of the corner of my eye. He was an odd fish, rushing home just because Mommy and Daddy told him to. "My mother's right, of course," I said carefully, so that he could not possibly misunderstand. "I've gone out with a lot of junkies in my time, but my current boy friend beats them all."

If I expected a reaction, I didn't get one. He merely said, "Then why didn't you go stay with him, or some other friend?"

"That's a good question," I replied. "A very good question." Then I closed my mouth tight. What was I talking to him for anyway? His wide, clear eyes made him look as if he'd scarcely ever smoked a joint in his life, let alone used anything else. An odd fish, that was for sure.

"Well," he said, "why don't you answer it, then?"

"Leave me alone," I retorted. "What business is it of yours, anyway?"

"Now we're even," he said. "You've butted into my business, and I've butted into yours."

I raised my hand in the air. "OK," I said, smiling. "Truce. Let's talk about the weather."

"What's your name?" he asked abruptly. "You can tell me that, at least, can't you?"

"Sure," I said. "I'm Nikki. That's short for Nicole. Who are you?"

"My name is Sam," he replied. He took a deep breath, and then he said, "Listen, Nikki, what do you think would happen if you didn't show up at your grandmother's? Would she be very upset? Is she meeting your train or anything?"

"No, of course she isn't meeting the train." I almost laughed at the idea. Who was I, a movie star or something, that anyone should meet my train? "I'm to take a cab to her place. Her office is having a party at some restaurant tonight. She won't be home until midnight, if then. She left the key with the super." I shouldn't have told him that. Doubtless he was a thief—a charming thief, like in those old black and white movies that were regarded as sophisticated comedies in their time, but a thief nevertheless. I glanced over at him. He seemed not to have noticed my remark about the key.

He flashed me his full, unadulterated, incandescent smile. "Then why don't you come home with me?" he asked. "You can just stay on to the end of the line." He spoke quite casually, as if he were Tony, who lived a floor below us and sometimes asked me to go with him to the bar on the corner for a drink. But he had put his hand on my upper arm, and he was gripping it in a manner that contradicted the unconcern of his tone. "Have dinner with me and my family. It'll be a lot better than eating alone. We live on a farm out in the country, and it's kind of nice. Then I'll drive you back to your grandmother's."

"That's silly," I said. "It's too far."

"No, no," he assured me, "it isn't. Don't let the amount of time it takes on the train fool you. It's only a forty-five minute drive from my house. My mother goes there all the time, to shop. There's a discount place there she loves. My mother adores a bargain."

"So does my mother," I said. It was probably the only thing they had in common.

I was tempted to accept his offer. All of a sudden I didn't want to be alone anymore. Not for another minute. I looked at him directly. "You promise you'll bring me back?" I asked. "This isn't some kind of con or something?" He wasn't the first guy who'd picked me up, but I had usually had some frame of reference in which to place the person. I had no hope that my life would improve. Who had hope in my world? But somehow, like a lot of other people, I dragged myself on. I hadn't quite gotten to the point of pushing that button labeled "self-destruct." I repeated my question. "You promise you'll bring me back?"

He laughed. "What do you think I'm going to try to do? Seduce you? In my mother's living room?"

Seduce. What an old-fashioned word. He was straight. Gorgeous and straight. "It's not seduction I'm worried about," I said. "It's rape that I can't stand."

"If you want," he said, "I'll sign an affadavit in blood. By midnight you'll be in your grandmother's house—if that's where you want to be."

"It's a deal," I said. "The blood won't be necessary. I'll tell you one thing. I didn't relish the idea of eating alone tonight. Not one bit."

He nodded, solemn now. "It's no time to be alone," he said.

"Because it's a holiday," I added.

"Yes," he said. "A holiday. Because it's a holiday."

Then the train halted at my stop and I didn't get off. I felt a delicious sense of adventure creep over me. The train no longer seemed like a vehicle out of a nightmare. It had become a cozy haven against the gloom of the deepening twilight. I settled the guinea pig's cage more comfortably on my lap, and then, as if of its own accord, my body readjusted itself so that I was seated closer to Sam. I had done crazy things before, but I hadn't usually felt good about them, they way I did now. I hadn't realized until I'd looked into Sam's face how very unhappy I'd been over the idea of spending the evening alone. "You don't think your mother will mind your bringing an unexpected guest?" I asked.

"You won't be unexpected," he replied.

"How can that be? You didn't dream of my existence forty minutes ago."

"I always bring someone home with me when I come for a weekend," he explained. "Always. They like it. They believe in hospitality."

"Girls?" I asked. I felt an odd twinge of jealousy. "Do you bring girls?"

He shrugged. "Girls. Guys. It doesn't matter."

"But this time you don't have anyone with you. Why's that?"

He hesitated briefly. "Someone was supposed to come," he admitted, "but . . . well . . . at the last minute, she changed her mind."

"Your girl friend." I pulled away from him and moved closer to the window.

"She was my girl friend." He had noticed my withdrawal, and he grinned. "Hey, she *was* my girl friend," he repeated. "You still have your junkie boyfriend, and I'm not mad at you for that."

"Well, I don't know," I said slowly. "I'm not so sure about Kenny anymore. I'm getting tired of him, if you want to know the truth, and I think he's getting tired of me too. That's why I didn't want to spend the vacation with him. We haven't agreed on much lately." I wanted to tell Sam all these things. I wanted him to know about me. I didn't want to fool him, not even if all we ever had together was supper.

And he seemed to want me to tell him. "What things?" he asked. "What things don't you and Kenny agree on anymore?"

"You know, I was pretty heavy into drugs myself for quite a while," I said.

"Yes," he replied mildly, "I know."

"Oh, no, you don't," I retorted sharply. "You don't know. You don't know what it's like unless you've been there yourself, and you haven't been."

"What makes you so sure?"

"I can tell. You've got people in your life who care about what happens to you. And you care about what happens to them."

"OK. Admitted."

I leaned back against the seat, satisfied. It was the first exchange with him that I'd won. "All right. So I was sort of freaked-out myself, like they say. But in the last few months, I've changed."

"Why?"

"You keep asking these unanswerable questions. I don't know why. I only know I began to think being stoned wasn't much different from being dead." I glanced at him out of the corner of my eye and then looked down at my guinea pig. "Lots of times," I went on quietly, "I think it would be a good idea to be dead. But I'm not ready for that yet, and I figured I'd stay away from ersatz death until I decided it was time for the real thing. Do you know what I mean?"

"I think so."

"Except for a joint now and then, I'm off the stuff," I told him. "But no one believes that. Why should they? After all, ninety-nine percent of the population is stoned seventy-five percent of the time. That's what it says in the papers. Everyone is just getting more and more stoned. But instead of the world getting pleasanter on that account, it grows more and more hopeless. Sometimes I think the whole world is like this train. It's going to grind to a halt any day now and find it can't get started again. One morning, nobody will wake up."

"Is that really what you think?" His voice was low and very serious.

I felt uncomfortable in the presence of such intensity. "Of course, I don't," I said sharply. "I'm joking."

"Naturally," he agreed, his tone lightening. "But let's suppose, just for the sake of supposing, that you're not joking. If the world really is like this train, and really does stop, what do you think will happen then? Do you think that will be the end, or do you think it will start all over again, from the beginning?"

I felt goose pimples form on my flesh. "I haven't studied metaphysics," I announced. Again, I reached my finger inside the cage on my lap and touched the guinea pig's long, coarse hair.

Sam laughed, and his whole face brightened. "You don't have to study metaphysics to ask metaphysical questions."

I knew that. I asked them all the time. I looked for meaning everywhere, and couldn't find it. That was my trouble. But I merely replied, "I'm just saying that everyone's stoned. You don't have to make a big deal out of that."

"It's you who's making it a big deal, not me," he pointed out. "I don't think everyone's stoned. I'm not. You're not. My mother and father aren't. Neither are my brothers." Then he checked himself and smiled a little. "Maybe," he admitted, "maybe Hamilton fools around sometimes, behind my father's back."

"Your father has a lot of control over his family," I commented. "That's kind of unusual."

"Well," he replied evasively, "we're out in the country, you know. Things are kind of backward out there."

"Listen," I said, "how country can any place so close to the city be?"

"You'd be surprised," he told me. "Did you know that only thirty miles south of us there are hundreds of thousands of acres of pine barrens, and hardly anybody lives there? Right in the middle of the most heavily populated part of the country we've got all this empty space. You just have to look for it, that's all."

"But you don't live there."

"No," he replied. "We live at the foot of the mountains. Maybe there aren't many working farms out there besides ours anymore, but you'd be surprised at the isolation."

"You don't want to be a farmer, though," I said. "You want to be a lawyer."

He took a deep breath. "I'm changing my mind."

"They're changing it for you. Your family."
Now I was sorry I'd said I'd go with him to meet

them. Sam's family sounded so unlike anyone I'd ever had anything to do with that I wondered if there'd be any common ground between us on which to base an ordinary conversation. I opened my mouth to announce that I was getting off as soon as I could and taking the next train back. But I closed my lips before any words came out. Unlike the waiting rooms at important junctions, suburban depots had poor security. I hadn't worn a helmet, and my gun was more decorative than dangerous. Any one of the roaming gangs that emerged at dusk would make mincemeat of a girl traveling alone. I no longer had a choice. I had to stay with Sam.

At the next stop, the train emptied out. There were only a few other people besides Sam and me left in the car. No one was talking; even the guinea pig was perfectly still. The lights grew dimmer and dimmer, until the other seats, the other people, were merely shadows. But Sam was real. I could feel the warmth of his body next to me. In the darkness, I fell into a sleep, a sleep light enough so that I knew when his arm slipped around me and my head fell to his shoulder. After that I slept more deeply.

The train had jolted to one of its countless halts when he gently shook me awake. "Get ready, Nikki," he said. "We get off at the next station."

"Is someone meeting us?" I asked.

"My brother Hamilton, probably," he replied. "He wouldn't miss the opportunity to drive his new sports car. It's imported."

"A farmer with a foreign sports car?"

"Why not?" Sam asked, reasonably enough. "But up until now," he added, "Hamilton hasn't been a farmer, either."

"What has he been?"

Sam grimaced. "When you find out, let me know," he said drily.

I took a tissue out of my pocketbook. The coach did have a toilet, but my stomach could barely manage the thought, let alone the actual sight of it. I wiped my face and hands, put on some fresh lipstick and eye shadow and combed my hair. It wasn't every day I had the chance to ride in a foreign sports car.

The mist was heavier than ever when we left the train, and thick layers of moisture hung in the air like smoke. Sam wore his knapsack and carried my suitcase. I carried my pocketbook and the guinea pig's cage. The station, a once-charming building of an architectural style popular a century ago, was now in an advanced state of decay. It was locked, and there wasn't a security guard in sight. We stood beneath a porte-cochere to protect ourselves from the dampness as we waited for Hamilton. "Just like him," Sam grumbled. "He'll insist on being the one to come get us, and then he'll stop to see fifteen different girls on his way into town."

"Sam," I scolded lightly, "don't exaggerate."

"I'm not exaggerating," he insisted. "Fifteen girls, plus a wife." He took his gun out of his pocket, released the hammer, and held the weapon loosely in his hand. "We may have a long wait," he commented.

I put down the cage and reached into my bag for my little ivory-handled pistol. The boyfriend I'd had before Kenny had given it to me for my sixteenth birthday. "You can put that away," Sam said. "I can manage."

But I didn't put it away. "Look," I pointed out. "Look over there." With my pistol, I gestured toward the group of half-a-dozen kids about my own age who were crossing the street directly opposite us. They wore the tight jeans and the leather jackets affected by most of the marauders who terrorized every village, every town, every city neighborhood. However, their jeans were pressed and patchless, their jackets the expensive suede variety. No hand-made Saturday night specials for them. The guns they carried were the best the finest sporting goods stores had to offer. It wasn't money they were after. They were just out for a good time. Which made them the most dangerous kind of all.

Sam was not concerned. "Don't worry," he said.

"They won't bother us. They're after easier prey."

Sure enough, an elderly man and woman had crossed the street from the post office that stood catty-corner to the station. They were heading for one of the taxi cabs parked at the taxi stand to our right. They carried guns, of course, but they never had a chance to use them. As the woman was climbing into the cab, one of the boys in the gang grabbed the old man from behind and pushed him to the ground. Instead of slamming the cab door, the woman made the mistake of turning around to see what had happened. Two more boys reached in, pulled her out, and threw her to the pavement next to the man. The old people's guns fell from their hands, and one of the girls leaned over to pick them up. Then all six of them started in with the usual business. Belts and chains appeared, and two of the gang members began kicking at the old man's face and belly. They were in no hurry to reach the climax.

The cab door slammed shut—the cabbie had reached behind him to accomplish that—and the cab roared away from the curb. Three or four other passengers, who had gotten off the train with us and were also waiting for rides, stood impassively under the porte-cochere, watching.

But Sam did an odd thing—a thing I'd never seen before. He walked over to the gang. They were so busy enjoying themselves they didn't even notice his approach. He grabbed one young man standing at the edge of the group, waiting his turn, and held his gun to the boy's head. "OK, "Sam shouted, "drop it. Get out of here. All of you."

The others turned, startled, and looked at Sam. "Shoot Willie," said the one who'd been working over the old man. "Go ahead, shoot him. Willie's one guy we can really do without. And then the rest of us will shoot you!"

"I'll get two or three more of you before you do," Sam countered in a voice so loud even the cabbies locked inside their taxis could hear it. "I'm the second best shot in the country." He laughed grimly. "You want to see my medals?"

The one Sam was holding, the one called Willie, began to shout too. "Bert, you make him let me go," he screamed. "If I'm shot, you'll have every kid on Southside Avenue after you. Don't you forget it."

One of the girls grabbed Bert's arm. "Come on," she said. "Let's go. We'll get this guy some other time." She pointed her finger at Sam. "I know him. He lives on a farm outside of town. One night we'll get him."

"OK, OK," Bert said, shaking himself free from the girl's grip. He gave the old man one final kick and sauntered off. Then Sam helped the old man and woman to their feet. The gang hadn't had enough time to do them irreparable damage. Sam settled them into one of the waiting taxis. Along with the other passengers, I watched silently from the sidewalk, our fingers wrapped tightly around our pistol grips.

When Sam returned to my side, I felt like shaking him. "What was the idea of that?" I asked angrily. "One of you and six of them? You've got no sense at all."

"And they have no nerve at all," he replied coolly. "Don't you know that?"

"Are you really the second best shot in the country?"

He laughed. "I don't know. I've never entered a competition. But I'm good enough. I've even gotten pretty good with a bow and arrow lately. One day I'll show you."

I shook my head. "Even if there'd been only one of them, you shouldn't have challenged them that way. They'll get you. You know they'll get you."

But Sam only laughed again. "Someone else will get them first."

A vandalized car, stripped down to its chassis, had been abandoned at the curb a few yards to the left of the spot where we were standing. Suddenly a thin, swift figure darted out from behind it. Before I was even aware of what was happening, skinny arms had grabbed the guinea pig cage resting at my feet, and skinny legs had dashed back across the wide street that separated the train station from an empty parking lot.

"Watch this," the figure's voice screamed. It was the girl, the girl who'd said the gang would get Sam some other time. By the light of the street lamp under which she stood, I saw that she had already taken the guinea pig out of the cage. She lifted him up as high as her arms would reach and threw him with all her force to the ground. Then with her feet, which were shod in heavy army shoes, she stomped on him three or four times. I thought I heard squeals, but at that distance I couldn't be sure.

Sam was already half across the street, after her. But she was quick. She did not linger. By the time he reached the guinea pig's crushed body, she was gone. He took a handkerchief out of his pocket and used it to lift the poor animal up and deposit it in the high grass that bordered the parking lot. Then, quickly, he came back to me. "I'm sorry," he said. "I would have liked to go after her, but I was afraid to leave you."

I was shaking. "Chase her?" I managed to say. "You really are crazy."

He put his arm around me. "I'm sorry about the guinea pig—sorrier than I can say."

"I hadn't known him very long," I replied. But the tears began to fall down my cheeks nevertheless.

I was glad it was too dark for him to see them. After all, who cried just because a guinea pig had died? Human beings were murdered in much the same fashion every day of the week, and each time it happened fewer and fewer tears were shed.

But Sam knew I was crying. His arm tightened around me. "Don't worry," he said quietly. "Soon it will all be over."

All over? What would be all over? I had no chance to ask him, though. A red sports car had zoomed to the curb in front of us. I wiped my eyes swiftly with the sleeve of my coat. Sam opened the door and sidled into the narrow back seat. I settled myself quickly in front, happy to be retreating into the relative safety of an automobile.

But Hamilton's first remark wasn't exactly welcoming. "Damn it, Sam," he said, "this isn't Phyllis."

"This is Nikki," Sam replied shortly. "Phyllis wouldn't come."

"Didn't believe you, huh?" Hamilton snorted.

"Didn't believe what?" I asked, annoyed. I began to suspect I was merely a last-minute substitute, a requirement for a dinner party that for some mysterious reason was necessarily arranged two by two.

Even though Hamilton had by now pulled away from the curb, he turned his head toward me again. "Sam hasn't told you?"

"Keep your eyes on the road, Ham," Sam interrupted sharply.

"All right, brother, play it your way," Hamilton replied lightly as he returned his full attention to the street and his steering wheel. Mist and black night had reduced visibility to nothing. It was perhaps this fact, and not a series of visits, that had delayed Hamilton's arrival at the train station. But I had seen enough by the overhead light that switched on and off when the car door opened and closed to realize that he was every bit as good-looking as Sam, though different. His hair was straight, not curly, and he wore it much longer. He was not as muscular, but slender and long-legged. He was just as dark-skinned as Sam, but his eyes were narrow and a brilliant green in color—devastating eyes, irresistable eyes.

"Nikki's not staying," Sam said. "She's just coming for dinner. Afterwards, I'll drive her to her grandmother's house." C881245 ᴄᴏ. sᴄʜᴏᴏʟs

"Dad won't like that," Hamilton replied.

"I'll talk to her later," Sam said. He tapped me on the shoulder. "Maybe I'll get you to change your mind, Nikki. Maybe you'll decide to spend the night. Maybe you'll even decide to stay the whole weekend."

I felt hot and oppressed again, as I had when I'd first boarded the train. Sam was stretching hospitality too far. And why did it matter so much to his father if I stayed or not? "Dinner is enough," I said. "I have things to do." What a lie that was. "My grandmother's expecting me." That at least was true, though the quality of her expectation was no doubt as questionable as mine at the thought of seeing her.

"You'd better tell Dad she's not staying," Hamilton said. "You better tell him as soon as you see him. You don't want him to misunderstand."

"Don't worry," Sam answered quietly. "I'll take care of Dad."

I wished that Sam were next to me and not behind me as the car hurtled through the blackness. Hamilton was going much faster than he ought, for instead of illuminating the way before us, the headlights seemed simply to reveal a dark wall of solid fog that threw the glare back in our eyes. Hamilton was silent, concentrating on his driving, and Sam was silent, too. Night and fog enclosed us so completely that I couldn't see a thing out of the window. I had no idea at all of where we were going, not the faintest notion of what kind of country we were traversing at such an unconscionable speed. With each mile that the car put between me and the town, my uneasiness grew. My stomach was queasy, and I could feel my palms sweating inside my gloves. What was I doing here, I kept asking myself, in this car with two men who were total strangers to me after all. I knew nothing of them. I wanted to cry out, begging Hamilton to stop the car. I would tell him that I was going to be sick. And then I would open the door and jump out and not get back in again. I might be a thousand times better off taking my chances with punks from a marauding gang who would behave in ways I could anticipate than I was locked in a car with two total ciphers. I'd hike to town and take the train back to where I belonged, back to where I knew what to expect.

But I remained as silent as Sam and Hamilton. I didn't open my mouth. I just sat there with my stomach churning and the lump in my throat almost choking me as Hamilton screeched around a corner on two wheels. Still I could see nothing. I was as lost, as totally without bearings, as if I'd been blind.

A moment later, from the sound of the tires, I could tell we had turned into a gravel drive. We proceeded for a moment or two longer, and then, suddenly, a large white clapboard house loomed surprisingly before me, the light streaming through its mullioned windows making it visible through the trails of mist. It was a handsome, square house, with black shutters, a spacious veranda approached by a short flight of wide, shallow steps, and a roof supported by tall round white pillars.

Hamilton braked in front of the steps. "I'm going to put the car in the barn," he said. "You two go on in." Sam took my elbow and led me up the broad stairs, across the wide porch, and through a white, paneled door with a handsome, fan-shaped window above it. In the foyer, I sniffed the welcoming odor of roasting meats and hot bread. The air was clear there, and warm. I gazed at the curved oak staircase and the highly waxed floor bathed in the soft glow of the lamp on the side table and the pewter chandelier that glistened dully above us. The lump in my throat melted; the queasiness in my stomach was gone.

A huge black, tan and white collie ambled into the foyer to greet us. "Hello, Angus," Sam said. He fell to his knees and embraced the dog, who licked Sam's face and wagged his tail in ecstacy. Then Sam stood up and called out, "We're here. We're here." I patted the dog too, and he licked my hand.

A man appeared through the same double doorway Angus had used. He was a tall man, in late middle-age, with a black beard and Sam's black eyes. He wore overalls, a flannel shirt and thick-soled work boots. There hung about him the faint, not unpleasant odor of the cow barn. Yet he was no hayseed. And it was not only his manner and his voice that attested to this. The big copper bowl of mums on the cherry-wood table, the old maps and the beveled mirror hanging on the wall, the richly colored oriental rug near the stairs—they were all evidence of the good taste of the people who lived in this house. I hadn't been in many rooms like this foyer, many genuine rooms. And everything was clean, so incredibly shiny clean.

"Dad," Sam said, "this is Nikki."

The man held out his hand to me and looked at me carefully, unsmilingly, but not unkindly. "I'm glad to see you, Nikki," he said.

"I'm glad to see you too, sir," I replied. When had I last called a man 'sir'? Had I ever?

"Nikki is only staying to dinner," Sam said quickly.

I thought I saw a slight shadow cross the older man's eyes. "I'm sorry about that," he said. "I had hoped you would stay longer."

"But you don't even know me," I protested.

"I would like to get to know you," he replied.

"Well," Sam interjected hastily, "perhaps you'll have the opportunity. But we can't rush these things, you know."

Sam's father smiled suddenly. "Sometimes we must, when there's so little time." I was at a loss to know what he was talking about, and my face must have told him that. "You'll understand in a while," he said. "Sam will tell you. Won't you, Sam?" It was not really a question at all, but an order. "I'm sorry Phyllis couldn't come," he added, "but no doubt Nikki will do just as well."

Sam nodded slowly. "I'm glad you approve."

Approve? I felt like saying: You don't even know me. How can you approve of me? And why should you have to? But I didn't say those things. I couldn't talk like that to Sam's father. Instead I turned toward the door.

Sam put his hand on the arm I'd stretched toward the doorknob. "Where are you going?" he asked.

"I'm sure I can persuade Ham to drive me back to the station," I replied softly.

Sam's father took a step toward me and looked directly at me with those heavy-lidded eyes that were so much like Sam's, yet deeper, and blacker. My own eyes fell away from the power of his glance. "Please stay," he said quietly. "I promise you, Sam will explain everything later. But stay now. I think you'll enjoy having dinner with us very much."

"All right." My voice had fallen into a whisper. Black sheep or not, Hamilton, I knew, would not directly disobey this man. If told not to take me back to town, he would not take me back to town, no matter what I might try to do to persuade him.

Sam took my hand. "Later," he said. "Later I'll take you to your grandmother's if you still want to go. I promised. I don't break promises." He turned to his father. "Trust me," he said. "You'll have to trust me."

I moved away from the door. "This is a nice

house," I admitted. When I had first seen it, I had felt as if I were coming home. But Sam's father frightened me. When he looked at me, I felt as if I no longer possessed a will of my own. The sensations of unease I had experienced in the car were creeping back. I was not surprised. It was typical of me to feel two ways about a situation at once.

Sam's father headed for the front door. "I'm going out to check the shipment that arrived this morning," he said. "Those animals aren't accustomed to this weather, and they may need some calming down. I'll see you later." He slammed the door behind him, and Sam led me toward the kitchen.

"What kind of animals?" I asked.

I expected to hear about cows, horses or sheep. But Sam said, "A couple of elephants, I think, and a pair of orangutans."

"Here? Are you crazy? What kind of farm does your father run?"

Sam laughed. "Not your regular farm, at least not for the last five years or so. Now it's a kind of game farm. He supplies zoos and safari trails and amusement parks—places like that."

"And the animals are here?" I asked. "They're all here?"

"Yes."

"That's wonderful," I cried. "I want to see them. Did you know that sometimes I go to the zoo and stare at the lions or the bears so long that I feel as if we're talking to each other?"

"I didn't know, though I knew you liked animals," Sam said. "We already have one like you in the family. My brother Jasper."

In spite of his denial, I remained half-convinced that somehow he had known. Lots of times I felt more at ease in the zoo than I did in our apartment or at school or at a party with my friends. "I want to see the animals," I repeated. "Every one of them."

"Not now," Sam replied. "It's too dark. There're so many creatures outside, the floodlights on the barns don't reach half of them. You can look at them in the morning." He grinned. "You see? I told you you'd want to spend the night. You can phone your grandmother."

I held up my hand. "We'll see," I said. "We'll see. Don't rush me. In the few minutes I've been here, I've changed my mind about this place so many times, I feel as if I'm on a merry-go-round."

We had entered the kitchen. It was a huge room with the most modern cabinets and appliances, but it was old-fashioned in its atmosphere. A fire roared in a fireplace made of mellow, rosy old bricks, and big black cast iron and stainless steel pots and pans hung from a rack above the stove. The walls were panelled in warm, dark wood, and the wide board floor was almost white with countless years of scrubbing.

A young woman and an older one were preparing the meal. Sam introduced the young one as his brother Jasper's wife, Katherine. The other woman was his mother. She was plump and very pretty, with carefully coiffed blue-gray hair that looked as if it had been done up at the beauty parlor that very day. Her apron covered a handsome camel hair skirt and silk shirt. "This is my mother," Sam said. "Her name is Na'ahma, but everyone calls her Ama. Nikki can call you Ama too, can't she, Mother?"

"Certainly." Her tone was pleasant, and she shook my hand with a firm, warm grip. "I'm pleased to meet you, Nikki," she said. But all the while her eyes were appraising me as carefully as if I were a new dishwasher or vacuum cleaner she was thinking about buying. "You can help us get dinner out. Another hand is always welcome."

My mother didn't cook much. If she ate home, she usually brought in pizza or fried chicken from a take-out shop. On the rare occasions when she did prepare a meal, I didn't help. But I found myself responding to Ama with a smile. "What can I do?" I asked.

"Set the table." She turned and addressed the other woman. "Katherine, show Nikki the plates and flatware. There are eight of us."

Eight. It appeared that both Hamilton and Jasper and their wives lived in the house, so it must have been seven that sat down to the table whenever Sam was home. Four times two is eight. I made eight.

"I'll go out and help Dad," Sam said. "So far, Nikki's just staying for dinner," he added with emphasis. "I'll talk to her about the rest later."

I wanted him to talk about the "rest" to me now, but I had no chance to ask. His mother got to him first. "Put on boots," she ordered. "The mud is impossible."

"If only it would freeze," I interjected, making small talk.

She glanced at me. "It won't," she said shortly. She turned her attention to Sam again. "I hope your father and the other boys have their boots on too. Now is not the time for any of you to catch cold."

Sam nodded and left. But before he was out of earshot, she called after him, "And don't forget to take the boots off again before you come back in the kitchen." She turned to me with a smile. "It's not so easy to keep the place clean these days."

"But this is the most immaculate house I've ever been in," I cried. "It shines."

"Well," Ama replied, "up until a few weeks ago, I had good help." She had two ovens, and she opened the top one to baste the roast. In the lower one a cake was baking. "But now, even Marnie's left me. After eighteen years, she's left me. Well, what can you do? No use railing against the inevitable." She shut the oven door again firmly and straightened up. "I never used to let animals in the house, either," she said. "I'm getting accustomed to them, though."

"We have to, don't we, Ama?" Katherine said gently. She had silently directed me to cabinets and drawers. I was laying out the plates on the long maple table in front of the fireplace. Off to the right I had glimpsed a handsome dining room furnished in a variety of antique styles, but I supposed it was saved for state occasions.

"I saw only one animal," I said. "That collie—Angus."

"Well," Ama replied, "of course I don't mean Angus. We've always had Angus. I'm extremely fond of Angus. After all, a dog is very nearly a person. I'm talking about the others."

I laid out well-shaped, heavy stainless steel flatware next to the plates. "I don't see any others," I said.

"Oh, not in here. Not in the kitchen," Ama explained. "That's why we're eating in here. Today Jasper put a couple of little cages in the dining room. I didn't even go in to look at them." She grimaced. "I think big spiders live in those cages. Jasper said they needed the warmth of the house." She looked at me apologetically. "I'm embarrassed, actually. It's not my way to serve company in the kitchen."

"Well," I said hastily, "don't think of me as company. If animals are your living, of course you have to take care of them. Anyway, I don't mind them—not even in the dining room."

She paused for a moment in her steady movement from stove top to oven to sink and looked at me. "That's fortunate," she commented slowly. Then she went back to her work. It seemed to me she was preparing a feast that would easily have served twenty —two kinds of meat, four vegetables, two home-baked hot breads, all sorts of relishes and preserves, fruit, potatoes and desserts I hadn't even glimpsed yet. And she was doing it without mussing so much as a single strand of her carefully waved hair.

When much of that food had been set out on the table, Katherine went out on the back porch and rang a bell. "Do me a favor, Nikki, dear," Sam's mother said. "Go up the front stairs, turn right, and knock on the first door on your right. That's Hamilton's room. Tell his wife to come down for dinner." The tone in which she said "his wife" was the same one she had used to discuss the spiders in the dining room.

I did as she asked. Two large snakes lay coiled in cages set side by side on the landing, and two gorgeous short-haired, blue-eyed cats were sleeping on a rug in the upstairs hall. I was glad to see them. My old alley cat, Purlie, had saved my sanity more than once, but he was dead now, and we lived in a different place, where all I was permitted were three turtles and two gerbils in a cage.

I found Hamilton's door and knocked. No answer. I knocked again, louder this time, and then again. "Who's there?" a sleepy voice asked at last. "Come in."

It seemed too complicated to identify myself. I simply pushed open the door. The room was dark at first, but in another moment, the owner of the voice snapped on the lamp on the bed table and sat up, rubbing her eyes. She was a tiny, pretty little thing who looked not a day over sixteen. Her sheer embroidered cotton shirt was all rumpled from her nap.

"It's time for dinner," I said.

She took her fists out of her eyes and looked at me. "Who are you?" she asked.

"I'm Nikki. I'm a friend of Sam's."

"I'm Lora," she replied. "Are you staying?"

"Just for dinner."

"No longer?"

"I don't think so."

She pouted. "I wish you would stay. You're

young. Everyone else around here is so old."

"Sam isn't," I pointed out. "Neither is Hamilton. I haven't met Jasper."

"Oh, they're men." She dismissed them airily. "I need another girl. Someone to talk to."

"What about Katherine?"

"If she's said two words to you, it's more than she's said to me in the month I've been here. She may not look old, but she sure acts old. She and her husband, old ladies, both of them." Suddenly she smiled. "But good-looking . . . wow! Wait 'til you see him. Sam and Hamilton are nothing compared to Jasper."

It was hard to conceive of a man better-looking than the two brothers I'd already met. "Maybe I will stay awhile," I said. "I'll see. But meantime, I think you'd better come down for dinner. It's on the table."

She wrinkled up her nose. "I don't think I can face another one of those monster meals. They make me sick."

"It looks awfully good tonight. Roast beef and potted chicken."

She bounced out of bed, wide awake now. "I'll throw up," she said. "I'm pregnant, you know." I could scarcely believe it. In her narrow jeans she had the belly and hips of a skinny eleven year old.

"Are you sure you're old enough to be pregnant?" I asked.

"I'm eighteen," she replied.

"So am I," I said. "I can't imagine being a mother."

She patted her belly proudly. "I don't look pregnant, do I? But I'm glad I am. I want a little baby. Once it's born, I'll leave Hamilton. I only married him because I was going to have the baby. But I'm sorry now. I want the baby to be mine, just mine."

"But it isn't just yours," I said. She seemed to me to be the stupidest girl I had ever met and less adorable with every word she spoke. "Nobody can make a baby all alone."

She shrugged. "Who knows if it's even Ham's? He wanted to marry me; none of the others did. It was funny the way he changed. He was the biggest swinger of them all, and then, bang, about a month ago, just like that, we had to get married and come to live here. We just had to, he said. Well, it's a crazy place, all those animals, and let me tell you, I'll be glad to be shook of it, once the baby's born."

She prattled on like a confiding child as she combed her hair and put some make-up on her face without even bothering to wash it first.

"The house is beautiful," I said, "but I can understand your not enjoying living with your in-laws."

"Ama's a witch," Lora said. "A blue-haired witch. And the old man is so solemn. He never laughs. Ham's OK though. He's better than any other boy I've ever had. Maybe I won't leave him, after all. Or maybe I'll get him to leave with me. Actually he's the only one who's ever been able to make me feel anything at all, and I've been having sex since I was twelve. How about you? Do you come?"

I thought I had encountered just about everything in the way of small talk, but I was startled by the content of this conversation, especially since the words were tumbling out of the mouth of an infant. She may have been eighteen, like me, but it seemed to me I was a hundred years older.

I didn't want to sound like a prude, so I chose my words carefully. "Look, Lora," I said as we walked down the stairs, "I like you and all, but I'm just not used to talking about that kind of thing. Not even with my best friend." I didn't have a best friend. "Not even with my mother." My mother would have been the last one, the very last one, I'd have talked about sex with.

"Oh, that's all right," Lora replied blithely. "I understand. I guess you're a virgin." That was a laugh. I swallowed hard and let it pass.

When we entered the kitchen, everyone else was already seated at the table. I took the chair next to Sam, and Lora sat down next to Hamilton. Jasper was there too. He was shorter than either Sam or Hamilton, and clearly somewhat older. But as Lora had told me, he was, if possible, even better-looking than his brothers—fair, like his mother, with enormously broad shoulders, a husky chest and eyes so blue and full of light that it was hard to stop looking at them. He appeared very strong and calm, like a rock. He spoke little, only now and then saying something to Katherine in a quiet, affectionate tone when he had the chance, which wasn't often. Katherine hardly sat down at all. The job of serving the meal seemed to be hers.

"Lora," Ama said, "I do wish you'd manage to get to meals on time. Everything gets cold."

"You don't have to wait for me," Lora replied through pursed lips. "I'm never hungry anyway."

"I know," Ama replied. "You don't eat enough to keep a bird alive, let alone a baby. Did you take your vitamins today?"

"If I feel like taking vitamins, I will, and if I don't, I won't." Lora's voice was petulant. "It's my child."

"And my grandchild," Ama returned sharply.

Her husband spoke then, his voice emerging forcefully from behind his thick, black beard. "This isn't an easy house to get used to," he said. "We must be patient with newcomers, and they must be patient with us." His eyes held his wife's. She lowered her glance, as I had done earlier when he had looked into my eyes. Then she nodded briefly.

Next, the old man did a very odd thing. It was something I had never seen anyone do before. He said, "I will now ask the blessing." All of the others at the table, even Lora, bowed their heads. "You too, Nikki," he said to me. I obeyed hastily. And then he said, "Blessed is the name of the Lord, King of the universe, Who brings forth the bread from the earth." When he was done speaking, we all picked up our heads. He broke a large chunk of bread off the loaf at his place, took a small piece from it, put it in his mouth, and passed the rest to his wife. She too broke off and ate a piece, and the chunk of bread went around the table, until all of us had eaten from it, including me. Then Katherine began to fill the dinner plates with roast beef, potted chicken and vegetables.

"Look," I said, "I don't want to sound dumb or anything, but who's this lord? This king of the universe who gives you your bread? Don't you buy it in the store, or bake it, like other people?"

"We have our own religion," Sam's father said. He spoke slowly and distinctly, as if he wanted to make very sure I understood him. "We worship the One God who created the universe."

"Which god is that?" I asked.

"The One," he repeated. "The One God."

"People used to worship gods," I said. "Lots of gods. We learned about that in Anthropology 101.

But I thought all those old superstitions had died out completely."

"We're old-fashioned," Hamilton interjected with a faint little laugh. "Very old-fashioned."

"It's not the same thing at all," Jasper told him sternly, "and you know it. The one true, just and righteous God, Creator of the universe, is nothing like those old gods, those warring and whoring old gods in pictures and statues."

"Well, what does he look like?" I asked. "This god of yours, do you have a picture of him?" I could take it back to my anthropology teacher. She would be amazed and delighted to find such a relic of the past, not in some isolated primitive village, but only fifty-five miles outside of the biggest city in the world.

"No, we don't have a picture of Him," Sam said. "He can't be visualized. He has no body, no form. He's a force, a spirit."

"All right, then," I responded patiently, "what's his name? He must have a name."

Sam shook his head. "I can't say His name," he replied.

"But Sam knows His name," Hamilton announced. "If anyone knows His name, it's Sam."

I shook my head. I could scarcely understand a word anyone was saying.

His father turned the deep intensity of his gaze on Jasper. "Don't look down on the old gods, Jasper," he said. "They were better than nothing. Nothing is what most people have now."

"But there is nothing," I protested. "For ages now we've known there is nothing. Any other attitude is totally absurd, completely unscientific."

Sam patted my hand. "In each generation there has been a scientist or a philosopher who felt different," he said. "No one listened to them, that's all."

"But you—you listen?" I asked, unable to keep my skepticism out of my voice."

"My father has received certain . . . certain messages," Sam said quietly, his fingers closing tightly around mine as he spoke.

I shivered, as if struck by a cold wind, even though the room was pleasantly warm from the great fire burning on the hearth. Had I fallen into a nest of fanatics? Was I trapped in a house full of cranks? I looked from Sam's brown eyes, to Jasper's blue, to Hamilton's green ones. And then I looked at their serious, intent father, and their good-looking, efficient mother. They weren't crazy themselves, but there was something crazy about them. I knew it. And there was something else in the house, something besides the people, something I could not understand. And that is why I shivered. My nerves were taut again, and my stomach queasy. Perhaps Sam noticed.

His fingers squeezed mine, and he smiled. Well, whatever else was in this house, he was in it too.

He changed the subject, on purpose, I suppose. "Hey, Jasper," he said, "when I first met Nikki she was carrying the oddest guinea pig I've ever seen. I'm sorry to say it came to rather a bad end, but I wondered if you'd ever run across any like it."

"What was it called?" Jasper queried.

"It had a name. Nikki, what was the name of that hairy thing?"

"*Cavia hirsutus*," I replied, barely managing to keep the sob out of my voice.

"No," Jasper replied, "I couldn't get hold of any. None of my suppliers had a pair on hand, and of course they don't exist in the wild."

"Well, Nikki had only one," Sam said. "That wouldn't have done us any good anyway."

"If he'd lived," I said, "a mate would have turned up for him eventually, if ever I had decided he needed one. What makes you think I'd have given him to you?"

"We'd have just borrowed him, Nikki," Jasper said in a gentle voice. "Just to get a line started. I'm sorry he's gone. Very sorry." I believed him. Unlike Sam, his interest in all animals, not just Angus, seemed more than academic.

Katherine got up from the table to clear away the main course. She nodded when she saw me rise, too, to help her. I knew I'd feel better if I did something, something very ordinary. I poked Lora's back with my elbow as I passed her. She turned her head, and I grinned at her. "Come on, lazybones," I whispered, "give us a hand." She rose from the table in a desultory way and began to carry dishes two at a time from the table to the sink."

"Well, well, Nikki," Hamilton commented when he realized what his wife was doing, "you're a good influence on Lora. You'd better stick around. We can use you."

All the men at the table indicated their approval of this sentiment with nods and smiles. But Lora, who was standing next to me at the sink, whispered, "You'd be nuts to stay here. If you stay, that would make you crazier than they are."

"I thought you wanted me to stay, Lora," I responded, reminding her of her remark to me earlier.

"I'd like it," she said, "but it wouldn't be good for you."

I was touched. I doubted that such generous sentiments came often to Lora's lips. I turned on the water in the sink to cover our conversation and began to rinse off the dishes, which I then handed to Lora to put into the dishwasher. Katherine was at the table serving cake, fruit and tea. "If everyone is crazy here," I asked, "why don't you leave?"

"I told you," Lora replied. "I will, after the baby. I can't now. Where would I go? My folks don't want me. Those homes for unwed mothers are awful places. I know a girl who went to one. She said it was like a jail. And I won't have an abortion. I want this baby. I've never had anything all my own in my life."

"Do you belong to your mother?" I asked.

"Of course not, the bitch," Lora returned swiftly.

"Then what makes you think?" I inquired, "that your baby will belong to you?"

"Because," Lora replied with absolute conviction, "I will care for it."

"I don't think we own what we care for, Lora. There's something wrong with that idea."

"Of course, we do," Lora said. "If we don't, what's the use of caring?"

I suppose, at the time, most people would have agreed with Lora. But I didn't, not even then. "If caring means owning," I said, "that makes caring back so expensive that no one does very much of it. I've never dared to do it at all."

Lora didn't answer me. She sauntered back to the table. I closed the dishwasher and followed her. We finished our dessert and tea. Afterwards, we all bowed our heads again. The old man said, "We have eaten, and we are satisfied, and we bless the Lord our God for the good land, which He has given us. So be it." Then he sighed, a deep, sorrowful sigh. All the others at the table echoed, "So be it." Then they all returned to ordinary conversation, as if nothing out of the way had occurred.

"Do you think it will start to rain tonight, Dad?" Sam asked. "The air's so thick with moisture it can't hold off much longer."

"Oh, it'll never rain," I interjected. "This damn mist is going to be with us forever and ever. I wish I were down south with my mother, where the sun always shines."

"Does it?" the old man asked with a little smile. "It *will* start to rain, Nikki," he added. "It'll start to rain very soon. If not tonight, then tomorrow. It'll rain down south, too. It'll even rain in the desert." He pushed himself away from the table. "I think I'll go into the living room and listen to some music. I shall miss music." I wondered where he was planning to go that even the sounds of a transistor radio would not reach him. "Would you care to join me?" he asked.

"Not to hear your stuff," Hamilton said. "How about some early rock, or even a little vintage jazz?"

"Come on, Ham," Lora said, "we'll go up and watch TV."

"I'm going to bed," Jasper announced. "Sleep's over for me once the lions start, and that's usually around five."

"I'll be up as soon as I'm finished in here," Katherine said.

"Would you like to see the greenhouse, Nikki?" Sam asked. "Some of the things Jasper has in there are kind of spectacular. You'll like them."

"Sure," I said, "after I finish helping Katherine."

"That's all right," Ama said. "Katherine and I can manage. You go along with Sam. You need some time to get better acquainted."

"You're right, Mother," Sam agreed. "Come on, Nikki."

Together we left the kitchen and walked out into the foyer.

"After I see the plants, you can drive me to my grandmother's," I said.

He didn't reply, but only smiled and led me through the living room where his father was putting a record on the stereo. Then we went through a kind of sun parlor and into a large greenhouse. He switched on a light. I felt as if I'd walked into a tropical dream. The air was damp, warm and soft, and my nostrils were immediately filled with the spring perfume of fresh, moist earth. Poinsettias, begonias and orange trees bloomed everywhere against a background of thick, lustrous green plants, most of which I could not recognize. I could only stare in silence, too busy breathing deeply to utter a sound.

"Jasper's hobby," Sam said casually. "Come, sit down."

We walked up a gravel path to the center of the room where the path widened and two wrought iron chairs and a glass-topped table had been set. I sat down and shed my sweater.

Sam didn't waste any time. "I'd like you to stay, Nikki," he said. "We'd all like you to stay—even silly little Lora."

"Why?" I asked. I shook my head. "Why do you want me to stay? I don't understand why anyone here should care if I stay or not. Your family's very nice, Sam, but frankly, there's something about them that gives me the creeps!"

"Don't you think it matters that you're able to say that to me?" Sam asked. "I never met anyone else I felt so much at ease with so quickly. I thought it was the same with you."

I admitted that it was.

"And then there are the animals," he said. "Tomorrow I'll take you out and show them to you."

There were animals in the greenhouse, too. Sam had shut the door carefully behind him as we came in. The chattering of birds and small monkeys filled the air, and furry little creatures scuttled across the floor. Here and there I glimpsed a butterfly or some other large tropical flying insect I couldn't recognize, and I was sure there were others too small for me to see. It was not just a greenhouse we were sitting in, but a total environment, like one of the glass-enclosed exhibits at the Museum of Natural History, except that everything in it was alive.

"Just stay the night," Sam went on. "Stay the night, and in the morning you'll see the animals." With a wave of his hand he took in the entire greenhouse. "This is nothing," he added.

"All right," I said. "I'll stay the night. Tomorrow you can drive me to my grandmother's. I'll call her later, when she gets home."

Sam grinned. "Good," he said. "Great! Come on." He stood up, grabbed my hand, and pulled me to my feet. "I'll tell you about the plants. Or at least I'll tell you as much as I know."

We walked along the path, frequently pushing aside the overhanging greenery to see what lay behind it in large red clay pots the tropical lushness of the growth hid from view. There was so much to absorb that I knew it would take days to really get to know the place, even with Jasper's expert help. Sam was no expert, but he made up for lack of knowledge with imagination.

"What's that?" I asked, pointing up to a hanging plant with slender, delicate reddish leaves and small pink and white flowers.

"Some kind of begonia," Sam said. "Jasper has about a hundred different begonias in here."

"And this is golden chain," I said, indicating long vines of sweet-smelling yellow flowers.

"That's right," Sam agreed.

"And this?" I cupped my hand around a brilliant blossom of deep scarlet shading into gold, which grew on a tall, graceful spike.

Sam regarded it for a moment, his face thoughtful and serious. "That," he said solemnly, "is a remarkable summer-flowering bulb called *tritonia nicola*."

I laughed, and he reached for my hand. "A perfect name," he said, "for such a vivid flower." We continued our stroll through the greenhouse, and he never let go of my hand again. We circled the place twice, and when we were again standing where the path widened, he pulled me to him and kissed me. It was a long, lingering kiss, as sweet and heady as the air that filled our lungs. My arms went around him, and I clung to him as if I were drowning.

At last our faces drew away from each other so that we could breathe again, but our bodies remained pressed together, and our arms were still entwined about each other. We smiled. "How can you ask why I want you to stay?" Sam murmured. "Surely you know."

I took my hand away from his back and ran it through his coarse thick black curls.

"Do you think you can forget him?" Sam asked.

"Him? Who?" I couldn't imagine who he was talking about.

"Your boyfriend. Ken. The junkie. Do you think you can forget about him?"

"Sure." I laughed. "I never got a kiss like that from Kenny. Of course," I added in an effort to be totally fair, "we never kissed in a conservatory either." I drew away from him a little bit. "What about Phyllis—the one everyone was expecting? Do you think you can forget about her so easily? Or are you a less fickle type than I?"

A shadow passed over his face, but in a moment it was gone. "As long as you're kissing me," he said, "the thought of her doesn't cross my mind." He bent his head to mine again, and we kissed many times, as if we couldn't get enough of each other, and his hands caressed me too, until there was no breath left in my body.

But that was all. I called my grandmother from the phone in the front hall. Everyone else had gone to bed. Sam said they had to because the lions woke everyone, not only Jasper, with their early morning bellowing. My grandmother was not upset that my arrival was to be delayed; I had known that would be the case. She didn't even question me as to my whereabouts. If I hadn't called, she probably wouldn't have noticed my absence.

Then Sam took me to the guest room where earlier he had put my valise. The house was silent and dark. There was nothing, nothing at all, to stop him from coming into that room with me. In fact, I never doubted that he would. Surely I knew enough to know he felt as I did, that there was something incredibly strong between us, stronger than anything I'd ever known before. Stronger and different. If I had to call what I felt when Sam touched me "attraction," then there was no word for what I had felt with others. It had been nothing.

So maybe I didn't know so much. Because if Sam felt the way I did, how could he just smile at me as he opened the door to my room, touch my lips lightly with his, and walk away? I stood in the doorway, dumbfounded, as if a pail of ice water had been dumped on my head. I was furious. How dare he lead me this far, and then leave me as if we had done nothing more than stroll in the park? I opened my mouth to call out to him, but I stopped my cry in my throat. What was the matter with me? Had I no pride at all?

I opened my suitcase, took out a robe, undressed, and put it on. Then I went into the bathroom to wash up. No sign of Sam anywhere. I returned to my room, shut the door, climbed into the bed and tossed restlessly for what seemed hours. I could not straighten out my thoughts. They ran around inside my head in wild jagged lines and refused to listen to my instructions to get themselves in order. I thought of getting up and smoking a joint, but I really didn't enjoy pot much all by myself.

Sam was playing games with me. He wanted me to stay, not because I was me and he liked me, but for some mysterious reason of his own. And he was not above using the attraction he knew I felt for him to persuade me to stay, or any other weapon at his command, like the animals outside he also knew I wanted very much to visit. That should not have surprised me. Everyone I knew was like that. But it did surprise me. Naively, I had expected something different from him. I had thought *he* was different. That's what I had thought.

It was very late, too late now to leave. Even if I got back to town, there'd be no train out at this hour. But in the morning, first thing, I'd go.

I looked at the phosphorescent dial on the clock. One o'clock. It had read twelve-thirty when I climbed into bed.

I turned my head away from the night table and resolved not to look at the clock again. Sure enough, eventually weariness overcame me, and, in spite of myself, I slept.

CHAPTER II

UST AS JASPER HAD PREDICTED, the bellowing of the lions awakened me at precisely five in the morning. Their noise was not a surprise. I felt as if I had been listening to it all night long in my sleep, but that I had not allowed it to waken me until morning. It was as if the creatures out there were speaking to me, directly to me. In spite of the plans I'd made before falling asleep, I knew I'd have to postpone my departure for a little while. First I'd have to go out to the barns and pay a courtesy call on all those who were living there.

The square of daylight visible through my window was as thick and gray as it had been when I'd last seen it, late the previous afternoon, on the train. I slid out of bed, walked barefoot across the wide board floor and leaned against the sill.

Outside, the rain had started to fall, just as Sam's father had said it would. I assured myself that that didn't make him any kind of prophet. It had looked as if it were going to rain for a week. It was coming down at last, and not in the large drops of a short-lived thunderstorm. It was a steady, persistent, pelting downpour, the kind farmers long for in the spring. Only it wasn't spring.

Rain or no rain, I would go out to visit the animals before I left. I washed and dressed and went downstairs to the kitchen, where I knew a cup of coffee would improve my spirits. I was very tired, but I would nap later, on the train.

Jasper had arrived in the kitchen before me, along with his quiet, watchful shadow, Katherine. They were already drinking coffee and reading the paper. Even in this isolated spot, it was delivered every morning. Katherine had the arts section, and Jasper was looking at the sports. The other two sections were lying on the table.

"Good morning," I said as I settled myself into a chair.

Katherine looked up from her paper. "Good morning," she said pleasantly. "Help yourself to coffee. Can I get you anything else?"

"No, thanks," I said. "I never eat breakfast. Do you mind if I borrow a piece of the paper?"

"Of course not," Jasper replied, lowering his section and looking at me over the top of it with a smile. "Whatever piece you want except the one I'm reading."

I poured coffee from the electric percolator and picked up the news section. I don't know why. Reading the paper was an increasingly depressing exercise. Everyone felt that way, which was why most papers hid the hard news about political and military events way in the back of the paper, filling the front pages with reports of what was for sale in the stores, amusing descriptions of high society parties, or the graphic accounts of murder, incest, child abuse and bestiality that fascinated most readers.

International events were relegated to the inside of the back page. I scanned the headlines. "FAMINE TOLL REACHES TWO MILLION. SURPLUS GRAINS ROT IN SILOS. BANKRUPT NATIONS LACK FUNDS FOR PURCHASE . . . 18,726 DEAD AND WOUNDED IN WAR'S 203RD MONTH . . . PRIME MINISTER HELD FOR MILLIONS IN RANSOM."

I picked up the arts section, which Katherine had discarded. "SOCIOLOGIST SUGGESTS NEW RENAISSANCE IN MAKING. FIVE ORIGINAL NOVELS PUBLISHED IN LAST YEAR . . . ROCK GROUP FINDS ORIGINAL SONG IN STAR'S ATTIC . . . LAST REMAINING LEGITIMATE PLAYHOUSE IN CITY CLOSES."

The business page was more cheerful. In spite of runaway inflation, department stores reported gross sales way ahead of last year's, and net profits too. The paper was loaded with gorgeous advertisements. "WHILE THEY LAST. HOTTEST ITEM IN TOWN. $2\frac{1}{2}$ INCH TV FITS ON SOAP DISH OR TOILET PAPER HOLDER. COLORS MATCH ANY BATHROOM DECOR." I knew they were selling out wherever they appeared, but I didn't want one. Like everyone else, I'd already seen every TV show. Two or three new ones a season were about all the networks had had the creative energy to come up with in the past couple of years.

I could read no more. I threw the paper on the table. Katherine lowered the page she was reading and glanced at me sympathetically. "Too awful, isn't it?" she said.

I nodded. "I don't know why I bother looking at it. Why do I want to know? Or if I do want to know, why does the knowledge disturb me so much?"

"Most people," Katherine said in her slow, thoughtful way, "don't know, or if they do know, they don't care. They really don't care."

"Which is as it should be," I said. "There is no other way. I know that." I sighed and sipped my coffee.

"But you feel sometimes," Katherine asked, "as if there should be?"

"Should be what?" I returned.

"Another way," Katherine replied. "Another way for the world to be."

"I think I'll drive into the city tonight," Jasper interrupted. "I want to catch one more hockey game."

"If the roads aren't flooded by then," Katherine said.

"Oh, that ought to take another day or two," Jasper replied.

"Another day or two!" I exclaimed. "You mean this rain is going to keep up for another day or two?" I reached out my hand. "Give me the weather."

Katherine pushed the page she had been reading toward me. I turned it over. "Rain all day today, tomorrow and Saturday throughout the entire metropolitan area," I read. "No clearing trend in sight at this time." I glanced at the weather map. The rain seemed to be established throughout the country, even in the northern tier, where one would have expected precipitation this time of year to fall as snow. Sam's father had said it would rain everywhere. Maybe he had called the weather bureau directly. Maybe that's why he knew about it. There was nothing unusual in that, I kept assuring myself.

As I looked up from the page, about to ask Jasper and Katherine what they made of the weather map, Katherine was watching me intently. Suddenly she put her hand on Jasper's arm. "Enough of this," she said. "Go get Sam. Nikki has to be told, and he's the one who has to tell her." Jasper looked at her for a moment. Then he nodded, stood up, and walked briskly out of the kitchen.

I turned to Katherine. "You tell me. I'm mad at Sam. I don't want to talk to him. But I do want to know what this place is all about."

Katherine shook her head. "No," she said firmly, "Sam has to tell you. He'll be down in a minute. Are you sure you don't want something to eat? It'll be good for you to eat something first."

"First?"

"Before you talk to Sam. It might take a long time. You might get hungry."

"I don't eat breakfast," I said again. "I never have. Why should I start today?"

Katherine pushed the coffee pot toward me. "At least," she said, "have another cup of coffee."

"All right," I said. I poured a cup for myself, but I didn't drink more than a couple of sips before Sam came into the kitchen with Jasper.

"Breakfast, Sam?" Katherine asked.

"Later," Sam said. "Nikki and I are going for a walk now."

"In the rain?" I asked.

"Yes, in the rain," Sam said. "I told you I'd show you the animals."

"I'd rather wait until the rain lets up," I insisted. I was being contrary with Sam. Actually, I had intended to visit the animals soon, rain or no rain.

"You know it isn't going to let up," Jasper said. "You read the weather report."

"I read it," I replied. "It doesn't say it's going to rain forever." However, I got up from the table.

"There're boots and slickers in the back hall," Sam said. "Come on." He took my elbow and propelled me across the room.

"After last night," I whispered, his touch flooding me with memory, anger and embarrassment, "I shouldn't walk one step with you."

When we reached the little room beyond the kitchen, he handed me a warm wool lumber jacket and a poncho from among the many that hung on hooks on the wall. "These may fit you," he said. "They're Katherine's old ones." He opened a wooden chest and pulled out a pair of boots. "Try these," he said. "I wore them when I was about twelve."

"Did you hear what I said?" I scolded, even as I was slipping into the jacket. "After last night, I shouldn't walk one step with you."

He looked up from his examination of the boots he was holding in his hand. "Why not?"

I was shocked. "How could you do what you did to me?" I asked in a fury. "What do you think I am? A stick?"

"No," he replied judiciously, "I don't think you're a stick, and I know for sure that I'm not one." Then he smiled at me, warmth and humor flowing out of his eyes and through me like heat from a fire.

"Then why. . . ." I began, blushing for perhaps the first time since I was ten.

"We're working from different premises," he said quietly. "We want different things. We'll talk about it—but later. Right now we've got to get outside. I don't know if any of the hands showed up this morning. Jasper and Dad may need us."

We finished wrapping ourselves against the weather, and then we walked out. It wasn't cold, only wet, silently, soakingly wet. The rain must have begun as soon as I'd fallen asleep. It was obvious that it had already been falling for several hours. We walked past the swimming pool, overflowing with brackish, leaf-spattered water. We walked on sodden lawns into which our boots sank, and then squished as we pulled them out of the mud. We walked through a narrow opening in a hedge. My shoulder brushed some branches, and water dripped on the olive-drab rain poncho I was wearing. I held my face up to the rain and let the soft, steady drops hit my cheeks, eyes, nose and lips until they felt as clean and rosy as a baby's fresh from a bath.

We were in the farmyard now. Corrals and pens were filled with animals of all kinds—ordinary horses, goats, sheep, ponies, cows, chickens, ducks, turkeys and donkeys. But there were others too—antelope, zebras, gazelles, elk, giraffes, wildebeestes, deer, lions, tigers, chimpanzees, bison, yaks, llamas, camels, gorillas, panthers, bobcats, wolves, leopards, cheetahs, boar, rhinoceroses and countless others, stretching as far as my eye could see. There were barns and stables, filled with more animals, I was sure, and temporary shelters made out of tarpaulins and tents that had been thrown up in some of the corrals. The animals were tethered, roped or separated by walls and fences. A low chorus of moos, growls, barks, screeches, rustles and snorts filled the air, but it was surprising how little commotion there was for such a crowd. Perhaps they had been tranquillized. I saw four men, one of them Sam's father, and another Jasper, moving among the animals, tossing hay and grain into feeding troughs.

"Good," Sam said. "At least Richie and Stash showed up today. Not enough, but better than no one."

"Why do you have so much trouble keeping help?" I asked. "Last night your mother told me all the household help had left too." I moved on before he could reply. I really didn't care what his answer was. I was more interested in the animals. With my nose, my eyes, my fingers, I wanted to absorb them all. I had been to both zoos in the city and to the ones in all the nearby cities as well. I'd been to every safari park and game farm in the area several times, but never, anywhere, had I seen so many animals gathered together in one place.

I went up to the fence of the nearest corral and looked at the pair of monstrous elephants tethered to two great metal pipes sunk in the ground. The ears of the bull were at least four feet wide and his tusks perhaps eight feet long. I had never been so close to such huge creatures before. There was nothing between me and them except a split rail fence. But I wasn't frightened. They were quietly picking up clumps of hay from the ground with their trunks and tossing them into their cavernous mouths, totally unperturbed by me or the rain or the other creatures sharing their enclosure. For a few moments I watched the gnu and wild goats and tiny red dwarf deer sharing the elephants' hay, the rain making their pelts glisten with a silver sheen.

Eventually I took my eyes away from the elephants and their companions. I looked up to the corral beyond, and to the corral beyond that, and to the one beyond that, and then, at last, to the fields beyond the last corral.

There was something at the foot of the hills that marched dimly across the horizon. I could not make it out. It was some kind of shape or structure, a looming shadow barely perceptible through the rain, its outlines blurred and indistinct. It wasn't a barn, it wasn't a stable, and yet I felt it was something made by the hand of man and not any kind of natural formation thrown up out of the earth a thousand geologic ages ago.

Sam had come up and was standing beside me. I turned and looked into his face. He saw that I had noticed the thing, the curious thing beneath the hills, and he answered my unspoken question. "We'll go look at it. We'll talk. I'll try to explain."

"The animals," I said. "I want to see the rest of them."

"You will," he replied. "Later. There'll be plenty of time. But now—that." He pointed toward it, and put his other hand on my elbow.

We began another journey through sodden fields. I pulled the string of my poncho hood tighter to keep the rain off my hair and set my gaze on what lay ahead of us. For several long minutes we walked as briskly as we could through the mud, and as we approached the thing, it grew larger and larger, its shape increasingly distinct. We were perhaps half-way there when I began to have some idea of what I was seeing. Yet I could not believe my eyes. I felt afraid, dreadfully afraid, with my throat closed by a lump and my stomach hollow again. But finally I could deny the truth no longer. I stopped walking and turned to Sam.

"It's a boat," I said.

"Yes," he replied quietly. "It's a boat. An ark."

I was shaking all over; every limb was trembling.

"We're so far from any water," I whispered. "How did it get here?" But I knew the answer.

"We built it," he said, as I had known he would.

We had long ago left the barns and animal pens behind us, but here, where we were standing, halfway between the house and the ark, there was another corral, all by itself, far from any of the others, set in a little copse. I walked over to it and leaned against the fence in an effort to gather myself together.

In the pen was a pair of unicorns, as white as snow against the gray day, with eyes as blue as a summer sky. I clutched the fence rail with my two hands and stared at them. After a few moments of gazing at them, I was no longer shaking. Sam stood next to me, but he didn't speak or touch me.

The male unicorn had a single fierce white horn more than two feet long growing out of his forehead, and a little white beard. The female had a much smaller horn, scarcely more than a swelling on her forehead. Their hooves were silver and they were about the size of a pair of ponies.

"I never saw unicorns before," I whispered to Sam in awe. "I thought they were extinct."

"Almost," Sam said, "but not quite. There have always been a few, a very few, in this neighborhood."

"And no one ever knew that?" I asked amazed. "No zoologist? No paleontologist?"

"We never made a secret of it," Sam said. "If

we mentioned it, no one believed us, that's all. We never pressed."

"Most people think they never existed at all," I said. "Most people think they're mythological beasts."

"Now you have something else to tell your anthropology teacher," Sam said with a little laugh. "Too bad you won't have the chance."

"Shh," I mumured. I knew how shy the unicorns were. I had read about them in old bestiaries in the library. I didn't want Sam to frighten them with his voice. I didn't want to leave them, though. They were a mystery, but after I left them, I'd have to confront the greater mystery of the ark. "It was wise of you to put them off here by themselves," I said quietly.

Sam nodded. "That was Jasper's doing," he said. "Jasper knows." Sam was allowing me this respite.

"How were you able to capture them alive?" I wondered. "The old books say no man can do it."

"Not as a rule," Sam agreed. "We'd never trapped any before. We'd only glimpsed them in the woods. But this time Jasper managed."

"I've read that they're very fierce," I told Sam. "Jasper should have tranquilized them, like the others." The unicorns were extremely restless. Impatiently, they paced their circular enclosure. The male lifted his head and sniffed the air with his long pink nose. Again and again he pawed the ground with his silver hooves. But when now and then the female stopped her skittish, fence-bound journeyings, she threw herself headlong against the fence itself, which was too high for her to jump. Or if she did pause to paw the ground, she, unlike the male, did it over and over again in the same spot, trying to dig under the fence. She seemed serious about getting out.

"The animals aren't tranquilized," Sam said. "No one's given them any sedation of any kind."

I didn't believe him. "They're all herded together," I said, "friends and enemies on top of each other. And except for the lions, they're all quiet. They wouldn't be so quiet if they hadn't been given something."

"They'll be herded a lot closer together before they're done," Sam said. "They're quiet because they know. All except these foolish unicorns. I can't imagine what's wrong with them."

"Maybe she left a foal somewhere." I suggested.

"Perhaps you're right," Sam said, his voice troubled, "but I hope you're not."

"What do you mean, they know?" I asked. "What is it they know?"

He took my arm again. "The ark," he replied. "You must come see the ark. Then you'll know what the animals know." He hesitated for a moment, and then he added, "I hope you will." His dark eyes were shadowed now, and his brow tense with thoughts I could not guess.

We trudged the rest of the way in silence. The ark loomed larger and larger before me until it seemed to fill the whole outdoors. I had never taken a sea voyage, but I had seen ships, of course, many times, docked in the harbor. This one was larger than any of them. Now that we were on top of it, it blocked the hills behind it, and I had to turn my head as far as it would go to see the ends of it.

"It's big," I said. "It's the biggest thing I've ever seen."

Sam shook his head. "Not so big," he replied. "Not big enough. But as big as we could make it. A hundred yards long, sixteen yards wide, and ten yards high. Aren't you going to ask what it's for?"

"No," I managed to say. The cabin roof was a brilliant red, the hull blue, the door and window frames green. It was as bright as a fun house at a fair, but it seemed dark and ominous to me. It was the product of madmen. It had to be, here, countless miles from any lake, any sea.

"It's for us," Sam told me, whether I wanted to know or not. "For you and me, and my parents, and Jasper and Katherine, and Ham and Lora, and all those animals. All those animals."

I felt as if my heart were being squeezed by a

great hand. Lora was right. She had warned me. "Why?" I whispered. "Why?" But I was afraid to hear his answer.

"Because this rain isn't going to stop," he replied in a voice as soft as mine. "It isn't going to stop until every person and every animal on this earth is drowned. Only those of us in that ark will survive the great flood that's beginning right now."

This time I said it. I shouted it. "Sam, you're crazy. If you think something like that's going to happen, you're crazy."

He grabbed me by the forearms. "I'm not crazy," he said. "I'm not." His voice shook with intensity. "You've got to believe me, Nikki. You've got to. It's true. God said so. God told my father."

"God?" I asked. "The one you invoked last night? He told you?" With all the strength I could muster, I shook myself loose from his grasp. I turned and began to run as fast as I could through the sodden fields, my boots, which were too big for me, flopping as I went.

But of course his legs were much longer than mine and besides, his boots fit. He caught up to me in a moment. "Please, Nikki," he said, "please. Listen to me. You must listen to me."

"You're crazy, Sam," I said. "You're crazy. I can't have anything to do with a crazy person."

"Ask my mother," he said. "Ask my father, my

brothers, their wives." Then he checked himself. "Well, don't ask Lora. She doesn't believe it, either. At least she says she doesn't. But she stays."

"What's the good of talking to them?" I asked. "They're as crazy as you are. Except for Lora, of course."

"Nikki, Nikki, darling," Sam said, "do you really believe what you're saying? Do you really believe that Lora is the sane one and all the rest of us are crazy?" He had grabbed my arms again to stop my running, and he turned me toward him, gripping me so tightly that I couldn't escape him this time. He took my chin in his hand and turned my face up so that I had to look into his eyes. "Do you really believe that?" he asked again.

He was right. How could I? How could I believe Lora was the sane one and all the rest of them were crazy?

"Come into the ark," he said. "Come in and just look at it." He dropped his hands to his side and just stared at me for a moment. Then he turned and began to walk back toward that great hulk looming behind us. Silently, I followed him.

We walked up a gang plank and onto a wide deck that completely surrounded the structure. Next to one of the several large windows was a small green door, which Sam pushed open. We entered the topmost of the three stories, or decks, which was also the smallest of the three. It was snugly and comfortably fitted for a long journey, with a large kitchen or galley, the chief feature of which was a huge wood-burning stove. Bedrooms and several storerooms were completely, if simply, furnished and stocked. This boat was ready to sail.

"You've gone to a great deal of trouble," I said somberly. "This god of yours must be remarkably convincing. If he spoke to me, maybe I'd be convinced too."

"He speaks only to my father," Sam explained. "You'll have to believe us. You'll have to."

I shook my head. "I don't have to believe anything."

We climbed down the narrow companionway to the lower levels. They contained stalls and cages for the animals, and a huge double door through which the creatures were to enter. There were storerooms here too, piled high with grain, and hung with dried meat. It took a long time to walk through the vast, cavernous spaces, but even so, I knew they were not big enough. "You don't have them all," I said. "You don't have every species of animal on earth. Not every fowl, every fish, every reptile, every amphibian, every mammal."

"You're probably right, Nikki," Sam said. "We have as many as we could get. We have to trust to God for some things. Those we don't have will evolve again from those we do, if that's what He wants. Or new ones—different kinds, if *that's* what He wants."

We climbed back up to the kitchen. A fire was laid in the stove and Sam lit it with a match. We took off our rain gear and our boots, and pulled two wooden stools close to the stove to warm ourselves. Sam began to speak. "Life will be very different afterwards," he said quietly. "We're taking along a few books and a couple of small musical instruments, but nothing else that you could call modern. In our new life, we'll have no power—no electricity, no steam. We'll have no source outside of ourselves to supply us with anything. We'll be starting over again, from the beginning."

For a moment I pretended we were engaged in a reasonable discussion. "Will it be different next time?" I asked. "Will the world be a better place the second time around?"

"I don't know," he said. "It may be entirely different. It may be exactly the same. Or it may be just a little bit different. God hasn't given my father the power to see far into the future. Dad only knows what's going to happen next."

"The whole world starting over again, from the beginning—"

"Not quite," Sam interrupted. "God won't have to undertake a new creation."

It was incredible. He believed his god had made the whole universe. But I wasn't going to embark at that moment on a discussion of the mechanics of such an event. I merely said, "Do you think the human race will have to go through all of this again?" My wide, wild gesture took in the whole of things. I didn't like the idea at all. It gave me the same feeling I had when I was a very small girl and went to the country for the first time. Walking out into the summer night, I had unexpectedly looked up at the stars and had felt as if I were sinking, sinking, sinking into weightless blackness.

"Maybe we'll come out a little bit better, just a little bit better, next time," Sam suggested. "Otherwise, wouldn't He destroy every last one of us and not allow even us few to survive to reproduce the human race?"

"He needs you to tend the animals," I said brightly. "To have to create so many of them all over again from nothing would be an exhausting job." The fire had warmed me enough. I stood up and put on my poncho.

"Now you're humoring me," Sam said. "Before, you were taking me seriously. I thought, for a moment, I had persuaded you."

I shook my head. "I'm going back to the house now," I said, "and I'm going to get my things. I'm going to leave here, even if you won't take me. I can walk as far as the highway, and then I can hitchhike. Someone will pick me up. I'll take this poncho and these boots. You owe me that much, anyway." I paused for a moment and looked at him. His head was down, and I reached out and touched his hair. "It was interesting," I said. "I'll grant you that."

Sam stood up too. "Now, wait a minute, Nikki," he said. "Just wait a minute. What harm will it do you to stay? If I'm right, and the world is destroyed, you'll be saved. If I'm wrong, you'll have lost nothing, except a few days' time. It's a long weekend anyway. You've got nothing else to do, and your grandmother won't mind. You'll call her before the phone lines go out."

" 'And how did you spend the long weekend, Nikki, darling?' " I imitated Melanie Marsh, whose activities were frequently reported in society gossip columns. " 'You're so pale. I guess you didn't go south, like the rest of us.' " I cocked my head and raised my hands like a princess in a marionette show. Now I was me, answering my blue-blooded acquaintance. "Oh, no, sweetheart. I didn't go south. I had the most delightful cruise on a boat that didn't go anywhere. It just sat in a sodden cornfield fifty miles from the nearest body of water, and I sat with it! You know, Sam," I continued in my own voice "you may be crazy, but I'm not, and I'm getting out of here while I've still got the chance. You must give me

Phyllis's address. I'll look her up. She and I have something in common. She refused to come with you, didn't she, when you told her what you had in mind?"

Sam nodded in glum agreement.

"Cheer up, Sam," I said. "You *are* attractive, incredibly so. That you got me this far is proof of that! After all this is over, you won't have any trouble getting yourself another girl. I'll tell you what—you can even call me, once you're cured of this temporary insanity. I assume it's temporary. I hope it's temporary. Obviously you can't all live in this ark forever. It already stinks to high heaven from the pitch. Can you imagine what it'll smell like once all the animals are herded in? When are you going to do that, by the way? When are you all planning to pile aboard?" Then I happened to glance into his stricken face. Suddenly my bright, ironic voice sounded shrill and unpleasant to my own ears, and I shut my mouth. I pulled on my boots. "I'm sorry, Sam," I said. "Goodbye."

I pushed open the little green door and walked down the gangplank. This time Sam made no effort to follow me. The rain hit my face as soon as I stepped out of the protection afforded by the overhang of the ark's roof. It was raining with exactly the same intensity as it had every minute since I'd gotten up that morning. I wondered what time it was now. Close to ten, I should imagine. But I felt as if it were midnight, as if I'd already lived through a full day, or several.

Head down, poncho pulled about me, drops of water pelting my back, I hurried across the fields, hoping to avoid conversation with any other members of the family prior to my departure. I supposed I'd run into one or another of them in the yards or the house, but I was resolved to keep the encounter minimal—no goodbyes, no explanations. I'd just leave. Let Sam do the explaining.

But I could not resist stopping once again at the unicorns' enclosure. They were somewhat quieter now. The female had given up throwing herself at the pilings and was concentrating on pawing the earth at her chosen spot near the fence. The hole had gotten quite deep. Soon there would be a space between the fence and the soggy ground. The male wasn't pacing either. He was standing quite still, watching her, raindrops dripping from his mane and tail. Every once in a while, he'd utter a soft neighing sound and nuzzle her flank with his nose. She paid no attention.

I knew unicorns were rare creatures, not only because there were so few of them, but also because they exemplified that other meaning of the word rare. Their nature was unusual. They mated for life. Few other creatures did.

I didn't know how long these two unicorns had been a pair. I had no way of knowing how old they were. But it was obvious that the male was extremely concerned about the female's behavior. I think he wanted her to stop trying to escape, to settle down and accept the predicament in which they found themselves. "At least," he seemed to be saying, "we're together. Nothing else really matters."

But something else very definitely mattered to her. She ignored his nuzzlings and his neighings, and singlemindedly continued pawing at her hole. I noticed that her teats were swollen now. I had been right. Somewhere she'd left a foal. It seemed not impossible that she would make a hole big enough to permit her escape, if not her mate's, since she was smaller than he. But it would take a long time. Before she succeeded, she might find herself in the ark.

I watched her for many minutes, almost as absorbed in what she was doing as she was herself. But then I remembered. I was leaving. Reluctantly, I turned away from the animals. Slowly I trudged back to the house, splattering mud with each step that I took. I saw Jasper and Hamilton coming out of one of the barns, but they were busy and only waved as I passed. I waved back and went on.

I entered the house by the back door and carefully discarded my rain gear in the hall. Ama was in the kitchen packing cardboard cartons with Mason jars full of pickles, applesauce and stewed tomatoes. Katherine was helping her. They both looked up at me as I came into the room. "For the trip," Katherine said.

I nodded, but I didn't say anything.

"Are you coming?" she asked hesitantly. Ama stopped her work and looked at me intently. They both waited, motionless, for my answer.

I glanced from one to the other, not wanting to tell them outright that I was leaving. I was convinced that Sam would never try to make me stay against my will, but I had no such confidence in the others. Katherine and her mother-in-law might easily fetch their husbands to restrain me. If they were all mad, they were capable of anything.

"Well," I said, "I don't know. I find the whole thing difficult to believe. I'll have to think about it."

"Would we have gone to such expense and trouble if it weren't true?" Ama asked.

"Oh, Ama," Katherine said, "that's not an argument likely to convince Nikki. Did you see that two-thousand-dollar tie advertised in the paper this morning? People spend fortunes on nonsense nowadays."

"Other people, perhaps," Ama replied. "Not me." Her authoritative tone left no room for discussion.

"I'll go up to my room," I said. "I'll think about it."

"There's nothing to think about," Ama responded. "You have to go. If you don't go, Sam will have no one. Later, that will be bad—very bad, especially since we're pretty well stuck with lovely Lora."

I didn't reply. I couldn't tell her that that reason wasn't any more persuasive than the one about the expense. I just nodded and walked out of the kitchen. Now I really was going to have to sneak out of the place. Well, they all seemed very busy. I'd find a way.

Upstairs in my room, I made the bed. Even if I was never to see her again, I wanted Ama to think well of me. I didn't want her to class me with Lora. Then I took the suitcase and began to put my things into it. Once more I heard the lions bellowing, and I went to the window to see if I could catch a glimpse of them. The window faced front, however, and no matter how far out I stuck my head, I could see nothing. I was sorry about that. I would have liked to look at the animals some more, but I didn't dare go out again. If I did, I might never get away.

And yet, I realized, that although I knew all of Sam's family were crazy, I wasn't really afraid of them. As Sam said, all I could lose by staying was a little time. Insane the human beings might be, yet for the sake of the unicorns, I was almost tempted to remain. But common sense triumphed, and I shook that silly notion out of my head, returning resolutely to the suitcase on the bed. I had barely closed it when I heard a tap on my door. Hastily, I shoved it under the bed. Then I called, "Come in."

It was Lora. She was just getting up. She wore a pair of absolutely transparent baby doll pajamas. This time I could see the rounded belly and enlarged nipples that gave evidence of her pregnancy. She plopped herself down on the bed. "Have you got a cig?" she asked. I gave her one, and lit it for her too. "Now, if I only had my coffee," she sighed, "I'd be perfectly happy. I'm really not human in the morning until I've had a cigarette and a cup of coffee."

I did not offer to go down and get her the coffee. She was perfectly capable of getting it for herself if she wanted it.

She took a few long, silent puffs on the cigarette. I sat in the little wing chair opposite the bed and watched her in equal silence. At last she spoke. "Do you have any pot?" she asked. "I haven't smoked a joint in so long."

I had a pocketbook full of joints, but I wasn't going to tell her that. "They're not good for the baby," I said.

"That's what Ham says," she announced glumly. "That's why he won't let me have any. I've searched the whole place, every corner, and I can't find any. I guess he really means it when he says he's not smoking either."

"Well, you see, if he can make that kind of

sacrifice, and he's not even carrying the baby, then you ought to be able to do it," I said.

There was a curl to her lip as she answered. "Boy, you sure had me fooled. I thought you lived in this century, but you're beginning to sound just like the rest of them."

I shook my head. "I can't figure you out, Lora," I said. "What are you doing here?" I paused for a moment and then added very slowly, "Saving yourself from the flood?"

"Do you believe that?" she asked. "Do you believe that crazy story?"

"Do you?" I retorted.

She answered my question with another. "Do you think I'm a fool?"

"If you don't believe it, there's no reason to stay here," I said. "They're going to lock you up in that ark any minute now."

"I figure that won't last long," Lora said. "It'll stop raining, and we'll all come out again. They'll look pretty foolish, and I won't let them forget it. But I can't leave. I told you I can't leave. On account of the baby." She laughed grimly. "They're stuck with me. Even Ama is stuck with me. You should have seen her face the day Ham brought me home and said we were married. She reached out her hand like she was going to slap his face. She would have, too, if he hadn't stopped her."

"Ham?"

She laughed even louder this time. "Him? Are you kidding? No. The old man. He's got his eye on me himself, I guess."

I couldn't imagine anything less likely, and I told her so. She was unconvinced. "He's always nice to me," she pointed out.

"Is that the only reason a man is ever nice to a woman?" I asked.

"The only reason," she said matter-of-factly. "And once he gets what he wants, he isn't so nice anymore. I mean, Ham's a perfect example."

"Ham isn't the only man in the world," I reminded her, thinking of Sam. There was no doubt about it. I was going to regret the loss of Sam.

But she wasn't listening to me. "They don't think I'm good enough for their precious sonny-boy. Well, I could tell them a thing or two about their darling Hamilton."

"I think they know," I said.

She continued along her own track. "The only thing he ever did that I couldn't understand was insisting that we get married, all of a sudden. And then coming back here and helping with the animals, and all that. As if he was like them. As if he believed in their ideas."

"You think he doesn't?"

She shook her head. "I don't know. He never

95

says he doesn't, but then, every once in a while, I catch him kind of laughing to himself, as if he's just going along with the joke. You know, I think Ham's afraid of his old man. Maybe he beat Ham when Ham was a kid."

Again I demurred. "He doesn't seem the type," I said.

"Well, whatever the reason, Ham won't disobey him. Not so he'd notice it, anyway." Lora stretched her slender limbs luxuriously and then jumped off my bed, graceful as a cat. She picked up the pack of cigarettes I'd left lying on the night table and dropped them in the pocket of her pajama top.

"Hey," I protested, "don't you have your own cigarettes?"

"I have them," she said smugly, "but I'm saving them. They may have to last a long time." And with a sly little grin, she bounced out of the room. And I had thought she was as transparent as her pajamas. Was it I who was the fool?

I leaned down and pulled my suitcase out from under the bed. I had made up my mind to go; I was going. Somewhere in the house I heard the clang of the telephone bell, the first time I'd heard it ring since I'd arrived. At our place, where only two of us lived, the phone rang every ten minutes. One of my mother's boyfriends had commented on it. "This place," he had said, "is as busy as a brothel."

"Nikki, Nikki." It was Katherine calling me. I couldn't imagine what it was she wanted. I shoved the suitcase under the bed again, opened the door and ran to the top of the stairs.

"What is it?" I shouted back.

"Telephone for you," Katherine said as she appeared at the foot of the stairs. "Your grandmother. You can take it in Dad's study. That's the room to the left of yours."

"Thanks," I said. Why would my grandmother be calling me? I had told her to warn the doorman I was coming so he could let me in when I arrived.

I went into the book-lined study and picked up the phone on the desk. "Hello? Grandmother?"

"Yes, Nikki, dear." Her voice was full of the empty, make-believe friendliness that represented all I knew of her. "Nikki dear," she went on, "something's come up. Could you possibly stay where you are for a few days? I'm terribly sorry, but this is an opportunity too good to miss."

"What do you mean, Grandmother?"

"I have an invitation to visit some friends who own a condominium down south. They just called a little while ago. Frankly, dear, it's what I was hoping for all along. You do understand, don't you?"

"Yes, of course."

"The people they invited first aren't coming,

because it's raining there too. But I'm sure it'll clear up down there faster than here, and at least it's warmer. I want to go. I'm so tired. You will forgive me, won't you?"

"Yes, of course," I repeated dully.

"Why don't you stay where you are, if they'll keep you. Or just go home. Your mother's left by now, and she doesn't even have to know until she gets back." My grandmother giggled, an absurdly girlish giggle. "You can do whatever you want by yourself."

"Yes," I said. "Well. Goodbye."

"Is that all?" She actually had the audacity to sound annoyed. "All you have to say is goodbye?"

"What do you want me to say, Grandmother?"

"I wish you'd stop calling me Grandmother. I've told you a hundred times, my name is Maureen." It wasn't. It was Mildred.

"We haven't even spoken to each other a hundred times altogether, Grandmother," I replied wearily. "What do you want me to say?"

"I want you to say, 'Have a good time.'"

"Have a good time. Goodbye, Grandmother." And with a bang, I hung up the receiver.

I could go back to the apartment. In this dreary, pouring rain I could go back to the apartment and spend the next week getting high with Ken. That's what I could do. Lots of coke and acid, and no sex at all. Ken was good for nothing when he was full of stuff, which was most of the time. That was my alternative to remaining where I was. I felt tears fill my eyes. I was going to cry. For the second time in as many days, old Nikki, who wasn't supposed to care about anything, was going to cry.

I marched myself downstairs. In the kitchen, Lora, wrapped in a negligee, was drinking coffee. Katherine and her mother-in-law were still packing boxes. Sam, Jasper, Ham and their father had just come in. Through the door to the back hall I could see them taking off their dripping slickers.

"OK," I announced in a very loud voice. "I'm staying. You may be crazy. You may all be crazy. But everyone out there is crazier than you."

Then I plopped down at the kitchen table, put my head in my hands and sobbed.

Sam was at my side in an instant. His hand was on my back, moving up and down, up and down, gently, firmly. "Nikki, darling," he whispered in my ear, "don't cry. Don't cry, Nikki darling. It will be all right. You'll see. Everything will be all right. We'll take care of you."

I had known he would say that. That's why I was staying. I picked up my head and snuffled back my tears. "But I don't believe that it's going to rain forever—"

"Not forever," Sam's father interrupted gently.

"Only forty days and forty nights."

"Whatever. I don't believe it's going to rain that long, and I don't believe everyone's going to drown. But I'm staying. You're crazy, but you're better than other people."

"Believe it or not, as you choose," Jasper said coldly. "The important thing is that you stay."

"Yes," Hamilton agreed. "Because if it should all be true, how boring it would have been for me with only Lora . . . and Katherine, of course." He winked at me and bent over to pull off his boots.

"Sometimes," Jasper said quietly, "I wonder why we have to take Hamilton and Lora with us at all."

"Is that how you feel?" Lora asked angrily. "Well, you better believe it's all right with me if I never again see the inside of that silly, smelly old boat."

The old man sighed. "We're all going," he said firmly. "We're all going, and you all know it."

A knock at the back door ended the bickering. Katherine went to open it. I glimpsed two men enter the house and stand in the back hall while Katherine returned to the kitchen. "It's Richie and Stash," she said to her father-in-law. "They want to talk to you." I could see them behind her, big hands hanging awkwardly at their sides, dampness rising almost visibly from their water-logged windbreakers.

"Come in, Richie, Stash," the old man called.

"Just leave your things out there," Ama added. "I made some fresh coffee."

The older of the two men stepped closer to the doorway leading from the back hall into the kitchen. "Come on in, Richie," Sam's father repeated.

"We just want to talk to you for a minute," Richie said. "It won't take long. It's not worth getting undressed for. If you don't mind, would you please come here?"

"I do mind, Richie," the old man replied quietly. "You've worked for me a long time. What you have to say should take more than a minute, after all these years."

"If you know what we're going to say, then we don't have to say it, do we?" Stash responded belligerantly.

Sam's father walked over to the men. "Come in," he said. "Don't worry about your boots. Sit down at the table. Have a cup of coffee. Once more, for old time's sake. You too, Stash."

The two men followed him to the table by the fireplace where Sam, Lora and I were already sitting. The three of them sat down, and Katherine brought three mugs and the pot of coffee over from the stove. But she didn't pour for them. She left the pot sitting on the table.

"We have to go," Richie said. "You know that. You've always been good to us. We stayed as long as we could. But they won't let us stay anymore."

"I know," Sam's father said. "I'm not blaming you. Don't think that, not for one minute."

Richie shook his head. "I don't know how you're going to manage. There're just too many animals. Why did you bring in so many? I told you not to do it."

"You know why I brought them in," the old man said. "I explained."

Richie held his empty coffee mug in his two hands, as if he were warming them. "I don't understand why you all went crazy at once," he said. "Now listen to me. I'm going to tell you this because you've been good to me. Tomorrow the sheriff's coming. They're going to try to lock you up. They're going to get you any way they can. They'll say you're crazy. They'll say you built that thing out back without a permit. They'll say you're keeping dangerous animals here. . . ."

"But we've always kept dangerous animals here," Jasper interrupted. "We've had a game farm here for the past five years."

"Nothing like this," Stash said. "You got to admit that."

"Jasper, don't you understand?" Richie said. "I always thought you were smart, and I was dumb. But now you're the one who's acting dumb. They'll get you on anything. They'll get you on anything they can think of."

"But why?" Katherine cried out. "What have we done to them? Why should they care? All of a sudden, why should anyone care what anyone else does? That's what I don't understand."

Stash stood up from the table. "I understand," he said. "I understand perfectly. You think you're better than everyone else. Of course, you're crazy, and no one wants a nuthouse next door. It's bad for property values, and dangerous too. But the real trouble is all your talk about how good you are and how rotten everyone else is. So if you'll just pay me what you owe me, I'll get out of here while I still can."

Sam's father reached in his pocket, pulled out a roll of bills, and began to count some of them out. He handed them to Stash, and then he said quietly, "Do you really think I think I'm better than you are, Stash? I've invited you and your family to come aboard with us. I've invited you a hundred times."

"Even though there's no room," Jasper said. "What you should have done is build your own ark."

Stash shook his head. "I'm not crazy. You are, but I'm not. I only stayed because the money was so damn good. It's almost too late now. I can't stay anymore." He turned to Richie. "If they find out you warned him, you're skin won't be worth a plugged nickel either."

"Are you going to tell them, Stash?" Jasper asked grimly.

Stash did not reply. He put his money in his pocket. "Well," he said, with a glance around the room, "goodbye. Goodbye." And then he walked past Jasper and Katherine, out into the hall and through the back door, slamming it shut behind him.

Sam's father turned to Richie. "And you, my old friend? Won't you accept my invitation to come into the ark? You and your wife and your son?"

Richie shook his head.

"You've nothing to lose," the old man went on.

"I've plenty to lose," Richie said, "and so do you. They'll carry you out of here tarred and feathered on the end of a rail, like in the old days. Or worse. And I'll tell you something else, whether you like it or not."

"What's that, Richie?" the old man asked gently.

"Suppose you're right. Suppose it really is the end of the world. I don't believe that it is for one second, but I'm just supposing. Well, I don't want to survive in a world where the only other people are this family. I mean, I like you and all that—or I did before this business started. But just you? That would be awful. You're just too . . . too. . . ." He stumbled looking for the right word. "Just too different."

Hamilton punched Richie's shoulder lightly. "You've got a point there, old buddy. I feel somewhat the same myself."

Richie's somber face broke into a brief smile. "Except for you, Ham," he said. "You were always more like the rest of us." He stood up. "I'm sorry about all of this. I really am. But I've got to go now, too. If you'll just pay me what you owe me. . . ."

Again, Sam's father withdrew the wad of bills from his pocket. He began to count some of them out, but then he stopped, rolled them all up again and pressed the entire wad into Richie's hand.

"Dad!" Lora protested. None of the rest of the family said a word.

"I can't take this," Richie said. "All I want is what you owe me."

"Keep it," Sam's father said. "I have no use for it. But don't hang onto it. Spend it fast."

"I'll hold it for you. When the rain stops and you're sane again, I'll give it back to you."

I thought it unusual of Richie not to take the money and run. Perhaps the old man thought so, too. "Are you sure you won't come with us?" His voice seemed almost to be pleading. "Are you sure?"

Richie solemnly pocketed the money. "I'm sure," he said. "Afterwards, I'll bring you your money, but I won't be able to work for you again. That's another thing I'm sure of."

The old man held out his hand. "Well, then, Richie, if that's how it is. . . ."

Richie took the proffered hand. "Yes," he said. "So long, and thanks—thanks for everything." Then he too was gone.

"Well, well, well," Hamilton said. "Now it's just us."

"I'm sorry," his father said with a sigh as he sat down again at the table. "I'm sorry but I'm not surprised. I was told that's how it would be."

"By whom?" I asked sharply. "Who told you?"

His voice was low and firm as he answered me. "God," he said.

"This god of yours told you everyone was going to drown except you and your family?"

The old man nodded. The room was perfectly silent. The others were listening with absolute intensity to our exchange.

"What about people already on ships?" I was trying to catch him out.

"If tidal waves don't swamp them, they'll starve, or die of thirst. It'll be a case of water, water everywhere and not a drop to drink." He smiled a little.

"And that doesn't bother you?" I asked in amazement. "The idea that everyone in the world will die except us doesn't bother you?"

"You heard Richie," he replied. "They don't

want to be saved. They don't want the world to be any different from what it is. I do. I want the mud and mire into which we've all sunk to be washed clean away."

"Even," I asked, "though all the people in the mire have to be washed clean away too?"

"I regret Richie," the old man replied. "We've worked side by side for fifteen years. But I can't save him if he refuses to be saved."

I felt as if an icicle had struck my heart. "You *are* mad," I said.

"No, I am not," he replied.

"Then your god is," I cried. "Mad or horrible. I'm glad I don't believe in him. I'm glad I don't believe in any of this."

Sam grabbed my hand. "But you're staying," he insisted, his brow creased, his eyes desperate. "You said you were staying. You're not going back on that."

I smiled into those deep black eyes. "I'm staying," I said. "There's you, and there're the unicorns, and then there's my own curiosity. . . ."

"And the fact that you've no place else to go," Lora chimed in. Had she listened to my phone conversation with my grandmother on an extension phone? I wouldn't have put it past her.

"That too," I agreed quietly.

"I've changed my mind," Jasper announced suddenly. "I'm sorry, but I think it's a mistake. If Nikki doesn't believe . . . well, that could lead to trouble."

Sam turned to his brother. "We have no choice, Jasper," he said firmly. "Do you understand that? We have no choice."

Jasper gave his brother a long, hard look. "All right," he agreed reluctantly. "I guess so."

"What about me?" Lora interposed. "I don't believe either."

"You just say that, Lora," Katherine said, "to annoy us. Besides, you're already pregnant."

"With Hamilton's child," Jasper added.

"You hope!" Lora murmured mischievously. But no one rose to her bait. I suppose they were getting used to her.

Katherine pulled up a chair and sat down next to me. "You know, Nikki," she said, "I've been troubled too at the idea that our god could kill off nearly his whole creation. But I think there may be other families like ours, in other parts of the world. We don't know about them yet, but maybe we'll find them, afterwards."

"Thank you, Katherine," I said. "It's nice of you to try to comfort me, but it isn't necessary. Since I don't believe this mammoth flood is going to take place, the whole subject, for me, is merely academic."

I turned to the old man. "I questioned you," I explained, "because I want to know what your god is like. I want to be able to tell my anthropology teacher about him, afterwards, when I go back to college, and Sam goes back to law school, where he belongs."

"I see," the old man said, no trace of annoyance in his voice. "Very well, Nikki. As you wish." He turned toward his wife. "Ama, we'll have lunch now. Then we'll all have to work outside this afternoon. There's still so much to do."

She scarcely seemed to hear him. "I can't stand to think about what's going to happen to Richie," she said in a low voice. "Just the way I can't stand to think about what's going to happen to Marnie. I mean these are people we've lived our lives with."

He put his arm around her shoulder. "I know, my darling," he said softly, "I know. But what more can we do? We've tried to persuade them. Now we must simply accept their fate, as we've accepted our own."

She shook her head dumbly. "Listen, Mother," Sam said, "they wouldn't lift a finger to save you."

"Richie would," she replied.

"The one exception," Sam went on. "But even he's content with things as they are. As for all the rest—every one of them—they'd as soon see you drown as breathe. That's the difference between them and us."

I interrupted him. "I'm them," I said.

He shook his head. "No, you're not. You think you are, but you're not."

"Oh, shut up, all of you," Lora cried out petulantly. "I can't stand this kind of talk. If you think I'm going to work outside today with those stupid animals, you're crazy. It's too cold and wet. Don't forget the baby."

"I'm not handy with the creatures," Ama said. "You can work with me, stocking the ark."

"I don't want to."

"But you will," the old man said. "We all have to do our share. That means you too, Lora."

"Ham," Lora appealed to her husband, "he can't talk to me like that, can he?"

"Listen, honey," Hamilton said, "it can't be good for the baby for you to lie around all day smoking cigarettes and drinking coffee. I think you'd better help my mother."

She raised her eyebrows and pouted a little, but after a moment she said in a low voice, "All right."

"Katherine and Nikki will work with us," the old man said.

"Yes," Katherine agreed.

"I'll be glad to," I said. "I'd prefer it. I'm not worth much around the house."

"We'll soon see how much you're worth out-side," Jasper commented drily.

And then we all sat down and ate our lunch. Quickly and silently, we ate our lunch.

CHAPTER III

Y THE END OF THAT LONG, WET afternoon, Jasper himself admitted that I had as much of a way with animals as he did himself. At first he set me to mucking out the stalls where the domestic animals were kept. But then, carrying my rake, I passed him, holding a hypodermic needle in his hand and hesitating at the gate leading into the pen where a pair of grizzly bears were in residence. Sam was with him. One of the bears was right inside the gate, rearing up on his hind legs, waving his front legs in the air and growling menacingly.

"Look, Jasper, forget about it," Sam said. "So this one won't be immunized. If all the others have had their shots, he can't come down with anything. There won't be anyone to catch it from."

"There'll be germs, floating in the air," Jasper said. "No mere flood will rid us of them!"

I approached the fence and began speaking to

the grizzly in a quiet, matter-of-fact tone. "Jasper's your friend," I said. "He's taking care of you, so you won't get sick. Just relax. Now just relax and let him in." I reached my hands through the fence, palms up. "Let him in now, big boy. Let him in." With my head turned up, I looked the grizzly right in the eye. He stared back at me, and then, lumberingly, he lowered himself to all fours and backed slowly away from the gate. Jasper turned and looked at me in amazement. "I'll go in with you," I said. "I'll hold him while you give him the shot."

"Are you crazy?" Sam asked indignantly. "That's what I'm here for."

"Let her, Sam," Jasper said. "Let her."

When it came to handling the animals, Jasper's authority was second only to his father's. I could see from his face that Sam didn't like the idea at all, but he made no further effort to stop me. "I'll go first," I said. I unlatched the gate, pushed it open and moved slowly toward the bear. Jasper came right behind me, closing the gate. Sam made a move to follow, but Jasper silently held up his hand to prevent him.

My hands were still out in front of me, palms up. I felt no fear at all, only a kind of joy, as if for the first time in my life I was doing precisely what I was supposed to do. I continued speaking quietly. "OK, big boy. Here we are. Here we are. Your friends. We're going to take care of you." What I said didn't matter, only the reassuring tone in which I said it. The bear remained perfectly still. I reached out and touched him. He did not withdraw. I began to scratch him behind the ears. "Now," I whispered to Jasper, "now." Jasper came forward and shot the hypodermic needle into the large muscle of the bear's hind leg. To such a huge animal, the shot was no more painful than a mosquito bite, and he barely flinched. "Good boy," I said. "That's a very good boy." I scratched him some more, and then we repeated the procedure with his mate.

Once Jasper realized I had a talent, he kept me busy feeding and calming the creatures who tended to act up. Even the endless varieties of skittish birds caged in some barns quieted down when I put grains and seeds in their feeding dishes, speaking softly to them all the while. There were no fish. The creatures of the sea, Jasper explained when I questioned him, would manage to survive on their own. Some varieties of insects too did not need the ark, but others he was taking along, like the spiders domiciled temporarily in the dining room, and the butterflies in the green-house.

Besides the birds, I had to deal with a pair of frightened lemurs, two nervous civets, some angry hyenas and the lions, who once again were bellowing their lungs out. Actually, though, the majority of the creatures were as relaxed most of the time as if they were safe in their own natural homes.

Dusk fell early, but we continued working because the barns and stables were lit inside and out. By the time we were done, I was exhausted and soaked through to my skin besides, but I was happy. All those creatures had warmed me.

I took an electric torch and went to visit the unicorns before going inside. They were too far away from the outbuildings and the other corrals to be visible in the glow of the floodlights. When I reached them, I saw that someone else had discovered the hole the female had dug, had filled it in again, and had surrounded the base of the fence with concrete blocks. She was pawing at one of them when I came, but she couldn't move it. It was too heavy for her, and she had no way of getting a grip on it. She whinnied at her mate. At first, he merely nuzzled her in response. I think he knew what she wanted him to do, but he didn't want to do it. Finally, however, her neighing and whinnying convinced him. He too began to paw at one of the blocks. He was bigger than she, and presumably stronger, but he couldn't move it either.

I took an apple out of my pocket and held it out to her through the fence. "Calm down, baby," I whispered. "Calm down. Everything's going to be all right." With my whole mind, I willed her to relax. But what worked with the other animals did not seem to work with her. The male came over, took the apple out of my hand and then nuzzled my arm with his nose. But the female went right on with her hopeless task.

I heard the squish of footsteps behind me. I turned my torch in the direction of the noise and saw Sam and Jasper coming to fetch me. "It's time to go in, Nikki," Sam said. "Dinner's ready.".

"You've been a wonderful help, Nikki," Jasper said. "I never would have believed it. You'll be invaluable tomorrow when we're loading."

High praise indeed, from Jasper. "Thanks," I said, "but I don't seem to be having much luck with the unicorns. The female is as upset as ever."

Jasper stood next to me at the fence and shone his own torch into the corral. "She's got a foal somewhere," he said. "It's too bad I had to take her. But unicorns are so hard to come by. These were the only two we even got close to. I saw from the beginning she was upset, but I couldn't find the foal, and I couldn't afford to pass the pair up, once we'd trapped them."

"You ought to let her go, Jasper," I said. "Really, you ought to. Before her foal dies."

"The foal's going to die anyway," Jasper said. "I intend to save its parents."

"It's probably dead already," Sam said.

"Not necessarily," Jasper explained. "Unicorns hide their foals and then go out foraging. If it's strong and healthy, the foal can survive a few days without eating. We caught this pair day before yesterday. They were the last species we took ourselves. That shipment trucked in yesterday morning was the only thing that arrived later."

Somewhere, not too far away, that unicorn's foal was sobbing for its mother, its cries growing fainter and fainter as its strength ebbed. I couldn't hear its cries, Sam couldn't, Jasper couldn't. But the unicorn could. I knew she could.

We turned and trudged back to the house. Through the rain we could see the golden glow that lit the windows with welcome. But I was not cheered by the sight. That foal was going to die because of a crazy family's insane idea, and I could not get the thought out of my head. Every bone and muscle in my body was filled with my weariness. I remembered suddenly that I had not gotten that nap I'd promised myself when the lions had first awakened me. That seemed like days, not merely hours, ago.

In the house we all went upstairs to bathe and change. I met Katherine coming out of the bathroom, her head wrapped in a towel, her body in an old flannel robe. "I shall miss hot showers," she said.

I took my own shower, put on dry clothes and went downstairs for dinner. The meal was much simpler than it had been the night before. Ama's only assistance in preparing it had come from Lora, and besides, I no longer counted as a guest. There was more than enough to eat, though, and plenty of wine. Jasper, Katherine and Ama drank very little, and Lora didn't take much either. She preferred other stimulants. Ham, Sam and I consumed our share. The old man drank the most.

"Dad, you better watch out," Ham said, his sardonic green eyes gleaming in the firelight as his father opened another bottle.

"I don't think you have to worry about me," the old man replied, without rancor. Indeed, neither his words nor his actions seemed in any way influenced by what he had drunk. "But I am going to miss wine."

"You'll have it again," Ham said. "I've put several different grapevine cuttings in the ark. I'm not trusting their survival to chance."

"To chance, Hamilton?" his father asked with a lift of his eyebrows.

Hamilton shrugged and poured himself another glass of wine.

"I'm going to miss hockey," Jasper said. "I thought I'd go into the city tonight and watch my boys one last time, but I'm too tired. I'll have to catch the game on television."

I felt warm now, and content, and satisfied with

my day's work, in spite of the unicorn. But the trend of the conversation unnerved me. "I'm tired too," I said. "As soon as we've cleaned up, I'm going to bed."

As I got up from the table, Ama and Sam also rose. "You worked outside today," Sam said to me. "We should help inside."

"Why?" Hamilton asked. "What difference does it make? After tomorrow, no one will be living here."

"I just can't leave the place a mess," Ama explained, an apologetic note in her voice. "I guess I just have to go on acting like I always did."

Sam seemed to agree. He made a pile out of several dinner plates and carried it over to the sink. Jasper, Katherine, Lora and I helped Ama, too. The old man announced he was going to listen to some music in his study and then go to bed. Ham disappeared; I didn't know where.

With all that assistance, we were finished cleaning up in short order. I went upstairs, took off my clothes and climbed into bed. I read for a few minutes, but my eyes wouldn't stay open. I fell asleep with my book still in my hand, the night table lamp still on.

In my sleep, I sensed that someone was standing over me. Then someone kissed me on the lips, and I awakened. Slowly, gradually, my eyes opened, and

I saw Sam's face above mine. He was kneeling by the bed. I smiled.

"I knocked," he said. "You didn't answer, but I saw the light beneath the crack of the door, so I just came in."

I was not awake enough to summon my defenses. "I'm glad you came in," I said softly. "I wanted you to come in. I wanted you to come in last night. Why didn't you?"

"If it was to be just . . . just a one night stand," he said, "well, that wasn't what *I* wanted."

"It's not a one night stand," I said. "It's not that." I moved over in the bed and pulled back the covers. "Get in," I whispered.

He reached over, took my book off the bed and laid it on the night table. He untied his robe, dropped it to the floor, and climbed in next to me. Then he switched off the light. He turned toward me and took me in his arms, and I felt his hard, warm body against mine. It was so lovely. It was the loveliest thing that had ever happened to me. And when it was over, I fell asleep. With my arms wrapped around him, I fell deeply, soundly asleep.

Later, something awakened me. I don't know what it was, but suddenly I was jerked into full consciousness. I reached for Sam, but all I came up with was a fistful of bedclothes. I sat up and turned on the lamp. Sam was gone. To take me with so much warmth and so much tenderness and then to go—I couldn't understand that. I wrapped the blankets close around me against the chill I felt in the air and lay back down. But I couldn't fall asleep. The lions were quiet. There was no sound at all except the steady, ceaseless patter of the rain on roof and windowpane. That sound usually soothed me. Yet tonight it did not. Every muscle in my body was taut. My eyes, wide open, stared straight ahead into the blackness. Bereft, alone, I felt as if I could not lie in that bed another minute.

I got up, put on my robe, and crept downstairs. The dog, the cats, the insects, even the snakes were used to me already and trusted me besides. They made no sound; they barely stirred as I passed.

But once in the foyer, I saw a light coming from the kitchen. I was not the only one who was awake. I entered the room and saw Sam's father sitting at the table with another bottle of wine and some cheese and crackers in front of him, a book in his hand. He looked up at me questioningly as I came toward him.

"I couldn't sleep," I murmured apologetically.

"Neither could I," he said with a smile. "Would you care for some wine and cheese?"

"All right," I said. Perhaps a little more wine would help me fall back to sleep. I got myself a glass from the cabinet and sat down opposite him. He pushed the bottle and plate toward me, and I helped myself.

"Do you want to know why I couldn't sleep?" he asked quietly.

"Yes," I said, surprised at his confidential tone.

"Because of what you said earlier," he told me. I was more surprised than ever. "How can God let them all die, even Richie?"

"Even the fat lady on the train," I said. How she had annoyed, indeed, frightened me when I was seated next to her. Now her memory made my heart ache. "You talk to him. Why don't you ask him?"

"One doesn't question God," Sam's father replied in a voice that conveyed the completeness of his conviction. "You can question, Nikki, because you don't believe. A believer can only accept."

"And lie awake at night."

"That I must accept too."

"Someday, maybe, someone will believe and still question," I said. "That will be good for your god," I added with some asperity. "He needs someone like that."

He looked at me, not with that glittering, inescapable eye I feared, but with curiosity and speculation in his glance. "Maybe you're that person."

"No, I can't be," I announced emphatically. "I don't believe."

"The one who can believe and still ask questions will be a better father than I am," the old man commented, his voice low and thoughtful.

"Sam, maybe," I suggested.

"No. It will take lots of time. It's a hard thing. Poor Sam."

"Why poor Sam?" He didn't answer me, but I realized that I knew the answer myself. "You mean because he can't find a girl who shares his conviction?"

Sam's father nodded.

"He really liked Phyllis, didn't he?"

"Yes."

"You all liked Phyllis, didn't you? She was more —more suitable than I, wasn't she? She would have fit in better."

"Less complicated, perhaps," the old man said. "That's not necessarily more suitable. I think you showed us this afternoon that you'll be far more useful to us, at least while we're in the ark, than Phyllis would have been."

"I wonder if Sam thinks so," I said. I had already cried once that day. I felt as if I were going to start again.

"Sam also accepts what is," his father replied firmly.

That was scarcely any comfort, as far as I was concerned. "I don't think I want any more cheese,"

I said. "I guess I'll go back to bed now. Maybe I'll be able to sleep." I didn't think so, but I didn't want to talk anymore.

"I'll go up too," he said. "I imagine I can sleep now myself."

We put the wine and cheese away and rinsed out the glasses. Then we climbed the stairs. When we reached the corridor, I turned to the left and he to the right. "Good night, Nikki," he said. "I really don't know how Sam feels about it, but I for one am glad it's you who's with us and not Phyllis." He smiled and touched my arm. He thought he was making me feel better.

I tried to return his smile. "Thanks," I said. "Good night."

"Sleep well," he replied. He moved off down the hall. The door to his room opened, and his wife stepped out into the corridor. The pale, rose-colored pegnoir she was wearing perfectly matched the floor-length, clinging nightgown underneath it. Together they revealed rather than concealed her fine, full figure.

She reached out and took her husband's hand. "I was worried about you," she said. "Couldn't you sleep?"

"It's all right now," he replied. He bent over and kissed her on the lips, and then with his arm around her, together they returned to their room.

She didn't even see me, and he had forgotten I was there.

Their door closed firmly. I went into the guest room, lay down on my bed and turned off the light. But no matter what I did, no matter where I put my mind, sleep would not come. I felt there was something I had to do. What was it? There was a hole in the middle of my brain, and an important thing had fallen into that hole. I struggled to pull it up again into my consciousness.

In a while I knew. I got out of bed and dressed quickly. I crept downstairs. In the back hall, I donned the old poncho and boots that I had come to think of as mine. I took a large electric torch from the shelf and stepped outside. Jasper had turned out all the floodlights when we had come in for dinner, and the house too was now totally dark. The only light was the one I held in my hand.

The rain was falling at exactly the same steady rate as it had all day. It had been pouring down for twenty-four hours now, and a week of mist had preceded it. I felt as if the sun, moon and stars had never been, as if sheets of gray, glassy rain were all I'd ever known, as if being soaked through to the bone were my natural state.

With difficulty I made my way across lawns and fields, past corrals, pens, barns and stables. Each time I took a step, I had laboriously to pull my foot out of the mud in order to take another. When morning came, herding the animals into the ark would be a nearly impossible task. Jasper and his father would have been wise to have done it before the rain started. But perhaps they had not been ready in time. Or perhaps they thought it best for the animals to spend as little time as possible in the ark's crowded, noisome quarters.

I had to laugh at myself. My mind was running on about the ark as if I really believed those animals had to go in there to be saved. I did not believe it. What I did believe was that Sam and his father and the rest of their family had given up the world's craziness for a private insanity of their own. I had consented to go along with it for a while, because sometimes it seemed a preferable madness—though sometimes it didn't.

I finally reached the corral where the unicorns were kept. I shone my torch into the enclosure. They had sensed my coming long before I had reached them. Earlier, weariness must have finally overcome them, and I think they had been asleep. But now, like me, they were wide awake, standing in the middle of their ring, their liquid blue eyes staring at me unblinkingly, their rain-soaked coats glittering in the light of my electric torch.

I unlatched the gate to the corral, walked in quickly and, without turning around, swung it shut behind me. I moved toward the creatures, my free hand held palm up at my side, the other grasping the torch. I whispered softly as I came, "Don't be afraid. Don't be afraid. It's only Nikki. Only your friend, Nikki."

They were the shyest creatures in the world, and they backed away from me as I approached. But their movements were firm and fearless. They were alert, their muscles taut with watchfulness, but they were not frightened of me.

I wanted to get close to them, particularly to the female. I wanted to put my arms around her warm, damp neck and pet her and tell her that I knew how she felt. I continued to walk slowly toward them, and they continued to back away. When they reached the far side of the fence, they began to move sideways. I pursued them, but carefully, quietly, unhurriedly, whispering all the while. Their retreat slowed. In a moment I was sure that I would be able to touch them.

And then the female reached the gate. She leaned her flank against it. Immediately, the gate flew open.

Instantly the unicorn realized that she was free. With one rapid, liquid motion, she whirled and trotted through the gate. Then, gathering speed as she went, she galloped off through the night like a streak of white lightning, so airy and swift that for her the mud was no obstacle. In a second or two,

I could not see her anymore.

I was nearly as quick as she. The male, startled, pranced back as I leaped forward. I grabbed the gate and shut it, latching it securely. Breathless, then, I turned and shone my light into his face. His mouth opened and from it issued a scream, a more than human scream. Every sorrow, every tragedy, every heartache the world had ever known was in that scream. My skin crawled, my hair stood on end, when I heard it.

Just once he screamed. Then he closed his mouth and turned his eyes to mine. They accused me. From their infinite blue depths, those eyes accused me. And rightly so. I had not secured the gate properly when I had come in. I knew that I had not latched it tightly on purpose. I knew it, and so did he.

Great tears formed beneath his lids and began to roll slowly down his milk-white face. I had not known that unicorns could cry. I had thought only people could cry.

I stood there, frozen, watching the weeping unicorn. As I looked at him, a terrible realization came over me. I began to shake from head to foot, as if I had been out in the coldest wind for endless hours. Then I knew. I knew that the world was going to end. I knew it for an absolute certainty. It was as if I saw the words incised on a rock. It was as if the unicorn himself was speaking them to me. The world was going to end.

The unicorn didn't take his eyes off me as I stood there shaking in the wind that came out of my own head. His tears fell like diamonds and mingled on his face, in the air, on the ground, with the everlasting drops of rain.

I gathered up all the strength of my will and forced myself to move. Pulling my foot out of the mud, I turned my body around and managed to make my hand grasp the gate latch. Its metal was cold, wet and slippery to my touch. I undid it. Carefully, I pushed open the gate. I moved so heavily I thought I was watching myself on slow-motion film. Holding the gate open, I turned my head and looked once again at the unicorn.

With one smooth, majestic motion, he lowered his head. When he raised it again, he was no longer looking at me, but instead staring straight ahead as he silently trotted through the gate. He passed me without a glance, without a sound. Then he broke into a gallop and like his mate before him was in a moment lost to my view.

What had I done? I didn't know. I only knew that the unicorn had to follow his mate. She meant more to him than life. He would bring her back if he could. If he couldn't, he would die with her. He knew it, and now I knew it, too.

I pushed myself through the muck, through the wet grass, through the sheets of falling rain. But I didn't really feel the wetness, although my well-soaked poncho by now provided little protection from the penetrating, needlelike drops. I was so lost in my dreadful, despairing, waking dream that though I shone the torch before me, I didn't see its light. I was not really aware of where I was going. The fat lady. Richie. The unicorns. They were all I could think of.

Nevertheless, I made myself move on. I made myself pull my foot out of the mud and put it down again in front of the other one, and then do the same thing all over again.

After a while, the edges of my mind became aware of something. I tossed my head, as if to free it from the black cloud that surrounded it. Once again my eyes began to see, to see through the rain and the darkness, to actually see what was in front of me.

I lifted up my head and swung my torch about me. I had walked away from the unicorn's enclosure, toward the ark.

And before me were torchlights, like the one I was carrying. There were several of them in the wide, empty fields to my right and to my left. They were all bobbing across the open spaces, converging on the ark, as if it were a dark magnet pulling them to it from all directions.

I heard no noise. Whoever was carrying those torches was keeping very quiet. I picked out at least ten separate glowing white spots. I hoped they were too busy with what they were doing to have noticed my torch. Or if they had noticed it, I hoped they thought it belonged to one of them. I knew they were also carrying guns. No one went out at night without one.

I doused my own light, turned around and headed quickly and silently for the house. I must have found my way in that bitter darkness by the sounds and smells of the animals. There was no light, not a speck of light, anywhere ahead of me. I tripped and fell over roots and rocks half a dozen different times, but I scarcely noticed. I raised myself up and continued laboriously picking my way across the fields and lawns. Now I was not merely soaked through, but filthy with mud and bloodied from scratches too. I think, though, that I actually went quite quickly. I was convinced that the torch bearers were up to no good. My anxiety swept everything else out of my mind. It carried me back to the house in much less time than the outward journey had consumed.

Once I was back inside, I began to shout. "Wake up," I cried. "Wake up. Wake up." I ran up the steps, my muddy boots leaving behind me a trail of black marks to mar the highly polished floor. "Wake up. Wake up."

My cries woke Sam first. He stood in his doorway, still tying the belt of his old robe, which fell scarcely to his knees, leaving exposed the muscular length of his bare legs. "Nikki, what's the matter?" he whispered. "What's going on here."

Before I could answer, Ham came out, zipping his jeans. Lora stood behind him, wrapped in a blanket. "Did you have a nightmare, Nikki?" he asked. "Did you take something before you went to sleep?"

The rest of the family gathered quickly—Katherine and Jasper in matching silk pajamas, Ama with a flowered cap protecting her bouffant blue hair-do, her husband already fully dressed. He strode unhesitatingly toward me and put his hand on my shoulder. "What is it, Nikki?" he asked. His glance took in the filthy disarray of my appearance. "What did you see?"

"There are some people out there," I said. "They're heading for the ark. About ten of them, I think. I don't know what they're up to. I don't think they saw me."

No one bothered to ask what I had been doing outside at that hour and in such weather. They bounded down two flights of stairs, into the workshop in the cellar where the guns hung in a rack on the wall. They all took one, except Lora. I took one too. Then, still excepting Lora, we went outside. She remained in the kitchen, huddled in her blanket, watching us through the picture window.

"Get the jeep out, Ham," his father ordered.

"But Dad," Ham protested, "if we're all in the jeep and they're scattered, we'll be sitting ducks."

"By now, they're not scattered," Sam pointed out. "They're in the ark."

Ham offered no further argument. He backed the jeep out of the barn where it was kept and we all piled in. "Ten did you say, Nikki?" the old man asked.

"Ten, I think," I replied. "I'm not sure."

"Good girl," he said. "Thank God you were out there to see them. I hope we catch them in time."

"What're they doing?" I asked.

"Probably trying to set fire to the ark. It won't be easy in this downpour. They'll have to do it from the inside. You did lock up after Ama and Lora left this afternoon, didn't you, Sam?" his father asked.

"Yes," Sam replied. "I pulled the shutters over all the windows. They'll have to use an axe to get in. It'll take some time."

Inside or out, they saw the headlights and heard the roar of the motor as the jeep approached the ark. A row of electric torches was strung out along the rail of the ark's deck, like a string of phosphorescent beads. "We should have snuck up on them," Ham complained. "Some of them may have escaped the back way."

"So what?" his father replied. "We only have to stop them, not catch them. What would we do with them anyway?"

"Kill them," Ham responded grimly.

"That's not for us to do," his father remonstrated, "—if we can avoid it."

Ham muttered something I couldn't catch, but he braked the jeep when his father told him to. As the vehicle halted, several shots rang out through the blackness. Ham had shut the headlights, so we were not an easy target, but some of those bullets came too close for comfort. Except for the old man, we all ducked, shielding ourselves as best we could with the sides and windshield of the jeep.

But the old man stood up. "Leave the ark," he called. "Leave the ark immediately." His booming voice was an awesome sound in the dark, wet, empty night. Even I, who knew perfectly well the source of the words, had the feeling that they came from nowhere in particular, from everywhere at once, that they surrounded and enclosed me.

I whispered to Sam. "I didn't know your father had such a powerful voice. He's better than any actor I ever heard."

"I didn't know it either," Sam admitted. "I

never heard him sound like that before. But he's done a lot of things lately he's never done before. You know," he added, "he's an old man. But lately, you'd never guess his real age. It's as if he dropped twenty years overnight."

I wasn't surprised. Nothing surprised me anymore. The old man raised his gun and fired a shot. I heard a scream ring out, and one of the lights fell. "Leave the ark," he repeated in that awful voice. "Leave the ark."

No one bothered with the man who had fallen. There were a few more scattered shots, but they fell far from their mark. The lights wobbled down the gangplank and dispersed over the fields in as many directions as they had come. "We should have set a guard," the old man said wearily, his voice his own now. "Stupid of us not to have set a guard."

We climbed out of the jeep and made our way cautiously toward the ark, our rifles at the ready, like a line of soldiers advancing in a battle. We didn't really know how many of them there had been. But they had not expected us to discover them, and of course they were basically as cowardly as the kids who had attacked the old couple the night Sam and I had waited for Hamilton at the station. Perhaps we would be lucky and discover they had all disappeared, except, of course, for the one Sam's father had shot.

We climbed up the gangplank to the ark's deck.

No light guided us, but Sam lead the way. He knew where he was going, even in the dark. Holding the rail, we carefully moved around the deck until Sam's foot hit something with a thud and he stopped. "Here he is, Dad," he said. "The one you shot."

"I think we can risk a light now, Sam," his father said.

Jasper had carried a flashlight up from the jeep. He switched it on. In its feeble glow we could see a body slumped on the deck. The old man knelt down and turned it over. Jasper shone his light in its face. It was Stash. The bullet had hit him in the stomach, and he was dead.

"At least we got one of them," Ham said with satisfaction.

"I'm sorry it was Stash," Jasper said. "He was a good worker. He really liked the animals."

"It makes no difference," the old man said without a sign of emotion. "We'll bury him later—if we have the time. Let's go in."

Inside we found oil-soaked rags shoved into the corners and along the floors next to the walls. Others had been hastily dropped in the middle of the rooms at our approach. We had arrived in time. Matches had not been set to them. That's the thing they would have done at the very last, to ensure their own escape.

But there was damage. In order to enter the

ark, the vandals had hacked away at the wooden door with an axe and gun butts, as Sam had said they would have to. They had known that from Stash, I suppose, and had come prepared. I wondered if Stash had been their willing confederate, or if he had assisted them merely to redeem himself in their eyes, because he had worked for the family long after everyone else except Richie had left. Poor Stash. Poor Richie. Poor fat lady. Poor Ken. Poor unicorns. Poor Grandmother. Poor Mama.

"We'll repair the door in the morning," the old man said, "when there's more light. Right now we better check the animals. They didn't shoot any. We would have heard that. But they may have let some loose."

"I think I'd have heard that too," Jasper said. "But you're right. We better check."

That was how they discovered the unicorns were gone—the unicorns and only the unicorns. None of the other animals had been disturbed. "I'll go after them," Jasper said. "Tomorrow morning I'll go after them or try to capture another pair."

His father shook his head. "There's no time," he said. "We must get on board tomorrow, all of us. Our neighbors will come back tomorrow night. You can be sure of that. Only this time there'll be many more of them. Well, tomorrow they can have the house. We and the animals will be safe in the ark. And after tomorrow, they won't come back. They won't be able to."

"The unicorns. . . ." Jasper began again.

"If the unicorns don't return on their own," his father interrupted, "we'll just have to forget about them. There are other species we're without, I'm sure. We don't know everything."

"The unicorns are freaks," Jasper said. "They won't happen again."

"It doesn't matter," his father replied. "It doesn't matter." How many times had I heard him say that? It was his watchword, the phrase with which he protected himself. I had no such phrase, no such protection.

Neither did Jasper. He was silent as we drove back to the house, but once we were indoors, taking off our wet things, I could hear him muttering under his breath, "If I could get my hands on the guy who let those unicorns out . . . if I could just get my hands on him. . . ."

"It was I," I said. "I let the unicorns out." Suddenly all movement stopped. Six pairs of eyes stared at me. The silence was absolute. I stood still and silent too, staring back, staring right at Jasper.

"I knew it was a mistake," Jasper said at last. "I knew it was a mistake to keep someone around here who didn't believe. If you believed, you never would have done it."

I nodded. "You're right, Jasper. But I believe now."

"You do?" Katherine asked. "How come?"

"The unicorn told me," I said. "That's the only way I can explain it. The unicorn told me. After I let the female out, the male told me. Then, of course, I had to let him go too. You understand that, don't you, Jasper?"

"No, I don't," he answered, his voice cold, his lips thin. "If I had only one to get, I'd have a chance."

"That's not true, Jasper," Sam said. He came over to my side and put his arm around my shoulder, as if to protect me from his brother's wrath. "There's no more chance of capturing one than two, since they always travel in pairs. We've no time left. If the price we had to pay for Nikki's commitment to us was the unicorns, then so be it." His arm tightened around my shoulder. "Don't forget, she saved the ark. She saved us all."

"I will never forgive you, Nikki," Jasper said implacably. "Never."

"I don't blame you," I whispered. "I shall never forgive myself." I shook myself free of Sam's arm, and turning away from them all, I ran up the back stairs as quickly as I could. I hurried into my room, slammed the door behind me and threw myself down on the bed.

But I was not alone long. Sam came after me. He didn't bother to knock, but burst into the room unceremoniously. He came over and sat down on the bed, putting his hand on my back. "Jasper doesn't mean it," he said soothingly. "That's not like Jasper at all. He'll get over it after a while."

I turned over and sat up in bed. "No, he won't" I said. "Why should he? The unicorns are lost for good, and he knows that there are no other creatures like them on the earth. They would die for each other." I was silent for a moment. Then I looked at him and asked softly, "Would you die for me?"

"Would you die for me?" Sam returned, his voice as quiet as mine.

I could not answer that question. Instead, I could not resist telling him what was rankling me. "You won't even spend the night with me."

"The bed's narrow," he replied, taking my hand in his. "We both needed a good night's sleep."

"Ah, Sam," I said, "next time people had better care more about each other. If they don't, the world will be just the same the second time around as it's been the first. And then what will have been the point?"

"I can't worry about that," Sam said, his firm practicality asserting itself. "I just can't. We'll have to go ahead, you and I, and do the best we can. That's all."

"Yes, Sam," I said, "you're right. I know you're right." With a sigh, I lay down again.

"You're exhausted," Sam said, his warm eyes troubled. "We all are. Try to get a couple of hours' sleep." He leaned over and kissed me on the forehead. "Good night, Nikki darling," he said.

I reached up, put my arms around his neck and pulled his head toward mine. I kissed him hard, full on the lips. "Good night, dearest Sam," I whispered. "Good night."

He smiled at me, infinite kindness in that smile. "Sleep well," he said. And for the second time that night, he left my room.

CHAPTER IV

HAD NO INTENTION OF SLEEPING. Sam had looked at me kindly, but it was not kindness I wanted. I waited for a while, until I sensed that the house was resting briefly before the flurry of activity that would begin in the gray and watery dawn. Then I got up from the bed. Carefully, I opened the door. I looked up and down the corridor. All the other bedroom doors were shut. Quietly I crept down the carpeted stairs, past the somnolent creatures, through the still, silent foyer and the dim, immaculate kitchen to the back hall.

I put on the poncho, rain hat and boots, still damp and muddy, though I wasn't sure why I bothered. They no longer provided much protection. Maybe I took them as souvenirs.

Stepping outside into the rain, I lifted my face up to the wetness and felt the cold, sharp drops lash my face. Then I lowered my head and started around the side of the house. I was making for the wide front drive that led to the road. I didn't know where I was going, only that I was getting away. I held Jasper's flashlight in my hand. Its little light would be sufficient guide for the journey once I had left the farm. Right now, the lights from the house and the floodlights in the yard glowed brightly. This time Jasper had turned them on, not off, when he had gone inside.

I came round to the front of the house. The walk was flooded, and some puddles were ankle deep. Before I started down the drive, I turned toward the house to look at it one last time, its yellow lights illuminating each drop of rain.

There, seated on the glider on the brightly lit front porch, was Lora. On her lap was the brass bell that Katherine used to call the family to dinner. She saw me as I saw her. "What are you doing outside this time?" she called to me.

I walked up onto the porch. "What are you doing?" I shot her question back to her.

"I'm the guard." She sounded quite proud of herself.

"You?" I couldn't keep my disbelief out of my voice.

"Why not?" she asked. "I did the least tonight, and I'll do the least tomorrow. If I miss a little sleep, it doesn't matter. If I see or hear anything, I'm to ring the bell."

"They trust you," I said.

"Yes," she replied. "Or at least they act as if they do. We must all trust each other now, the old man says. We have no other choice."

"So you do believe," I said. "You believed all along."

"You believe now, too," she responded simply.

I sat down next to her on the glider. "Yes," I said, "I do. And that's why I'm leaving. Can you understand that?"

She shook her head.

"Sam doesn't care about me," I explained. "He wants me to come along because I'm good with animals. He knew that from the moment he first saw me on the train."

"He was with you tonight," Lora said. "I know that. Didn't you like it?"

"Of course I liked it," I replied indignantly. Was sex all that mattered to her? "He's Sam, after all. But he came to me because he knew I wanted him, and he thought that would be one way to make sure I'd stay. Only for me it's not enough. Nor for him either, really. There must be someone else around that he can take along. Someone better than me. Someone he can really care about."

"What nonsense," she replied shortly.

"Or maybe Katherine's right," I went on. "Maybe there are others somewhere who will be saved, and he'll find one of them when the ark finally goes aground on some faraway mountain peak." I looked at her, but her face was still as stone. "Or he'll have nieces," I continued, "and they'll grow up, and under the circumstances, that'll be all right. There's got to be something better than me for him."

"And nothing for you?" Lora asked.

"I'd rather die with the others." I felt as if the admission were being wrung from me, like dirty water from a mop.

"Did you tell Sam you were leaving?" she asked.

"He doesn't want me to stay against my will," I equivocated. "You know that."

"But you didn't tell him you were going," she persisted.

I nodded mutely.

She drew back into the corner of the glider. "And you," she said, "you had the nerve to look down on me!"

"Don't ring your bell, Lora," I begged. "Please don't ring that bell."

"Don't worry," she replied, her lip curling with disdain, "I won't. Sam will be better off alone than stuck with you and your complicated ideas."

"Scruples, I guess you'd call them," I said. "You're right, Lora, of course. You'll all be better off without me, particularly Sam. I can't face this family's future. I simply can't face it. I don't belong with them. I belong with the other people. With Richie, and the fat lady, and the unicorns."

"I don't know what you're talking about," Lora said. Then she smiled a little, adding speculatively, "But I'll tell you one thing. I like Sam. He's even more attractive than Ham. And of course, Jasper is the best-looking one of all. . . ."

"Then you won't say anything?"

"Not until I'm asked. They told me to warn them if anyone came in, but no one said anything about anyone going out. I won't lie, though. If they ask me, I won't lie."

"All right, Lora. That's good enough." I stood up. "Goodbye." I almost extended my hand to her, but then I thought better of it.

"Goodbye," she replied quietly.

I left the porch and began to walk down the drive. Like the flagstone pathway, it was full of puddles. In another few hours, it would be a stream. I splashed along, turning back only once to glance at the house. Lora sat there, like a statue, in the corner of the glider, the brass bell on her lap.

The drive was at least a quarter mile long. It was a while before I reached the end of it. Then I turned into the road. It too was full of deep puddles —pools would be a better word to describe the accumulations of water through which I had to navigate. In places the road was already impassible to vehicles, though I, on foot, not caring how wet I got, could still make my way.

After about an hour, I reached the highway. Tramping and splashing along, the rain running in rivulets down my cheeks and pelting my back, I had thought I might try to get to my grandmother's place or go back to my mother's apartment in the city. I no longer thought of it as home. Home was the handsome farmhouse I had just left. Still, the apartment was a place to go, and I had to go somewhere. I had thought too of finding Ken so I wouldn't be by myself when the end came. But I had changed my mind about that. If I couldn't be with the people who had come to matter the most to me, I would be better off alone. I'd find a cat or dog to keep me company.

But once I reached the highway, I realized that going anywhere any way except on foot was easier to contemplate than to do. There were no vehicles traveling on the road—there wouldn't have been many at such an early hour in any case. But there were cars abandoned on the shoulder, water up to their hubcaps. The highway, lying low in a kind of valley in an area where extensive overdevelopment had destroyed the flood plain, was already impassible. Thirty-six hours of steady, ceaseless rain had been enough to accomplish that.

The fields along the side of the highway were

flooded too. I could wade through, and perhaps reach a higher, drier place, but to what end? I was never going to make it even as far as the railroad station in town.

I could go back the way I had come. Maybe Richie lived along that road somewhere. Maybe he and his wife would take me in. But in truth, the chance of finding Richie was small. He could live anywhere. I knew no one else out here, no one at all. No one would take in a stranger. Most people wouldn't even take in someone they knew.

The traffic light at the crossroads at which I stood gleamed in the night, turning from red to green to yellow and back to red again. All of a sudden I started to laugh hysterically, the sound of my crazy laughter rising above the steady patter of the rain. The sight of that light, directing non-existent traffic, traffic that would never roll again, was suddenly too funny to bear. And then, while I stood there laughing, the traffic light went dark. Everything was ending so soon—so much sooner than I had expected.

I stopped laughing as suddenly as I had started. There was a little shopping center at the crossroads —a supermarket, a liquor store, a pharmacy, a drug shop, a laundromat. I splashed through the water, looking in one abandoned car after another until I found one with the keys still in the ignition. I opened the door, took the keys, used them to open the car's trunk and extricated the jack from under the water that had accumulated on the trunk floor. I used the jack to break the plate glass window in the super-market, and then I went inside. At least I wouldn't starve to death.

I tried the light switches, but they didn't work. All the power was out now, I supposed, the lines too wet to carry it. I used what was left of my flashlight to find other flashlights, batteries, candles and matches before Jasper's light died completely. The floor of the market was still dry. The water seemed as yet to be confined to the basement.

Then I gathered some supplies together—can-ned goods, a can opener, soda in bottles, bread, cakes, cookies, dry clothes, instant coffee, a Pyrex pot with a candle warmer, some fruit and vegetables. In the back of the supermarket I found the office. Going in and shuting the door behind me, I stripped myself of my wet things and dressed in a couple of layers of underclothing, the biggest cheap imported shirt I'd been able to find, socks and bedroom slippers. I must have looked like a visitor from another planet, but I was not, after all, expecting a photographer from a fashion magazine.

There was an old Naugahyde club chair in the office. After I'd eaten an apple, I curled up in it, covered myself with some butcher coats I had dis-covered piled on a shelf, and fell asleep. My last thought as I drifted off was that I wished the supermarket had a cat. I would have liked a cat sleeping on my feet.

By the time I woke up, day had broken—or as much day as we were going to get. I didn't waken of my own accord. I was so exhausted that left to myself I would have slept for hours, maybe until I drowned in my sleep. But there had been a noise, a loud noise. Had some of the market employees managed to make it to work in spite of the flooding? I hadn't expected that.

I got up out of the chair, aching all over from sleeping in such an awkward position and stretched my chilled limbs one by one. Then I opened the office door and peeked out into the market proper. It was a huge place, and I saw nothing. I walked out of the office and down the aisle full of paper towels, paper cups and paper napkins on one side, and dog food, cat food and kitty litter on the other. There was an icy dampness in the air, no doubt from the window I had broken to get in.

Something else had come in too. It was he who had made the noise that I had heard, and when I got to the front of the store, I saw him standing at the end of one of the checkout aisles, looking about him with his great blue eyes, sniffing the air with his long pale nose. It was the unicorn.

As soon as he saw me, he came limping over.

There was a bad cut on his right front foreleg. Perhaps he had acquired it jumping through the jagged glass of the broken window. His legs were full of mud, and his flanks were wet and spattered, too.

I met him halfway and held out my hand to him. He put his nose in my palm and licked it with his wet, rough tongue; then he put his head beneath my arm and nuzzled my side. I stroked his neck and kissed him on the forehead on either side of his horn. But he needed more than that. I found a package of dish-towels, which I tore open, and cleaned him up as best I could without any water. How odd to be without water under the circumstances. Then I bathed his wound with disinfectant and bandaged it with gauze and tape. The supermarket had everything, of course. That was the nature of supermarkets.

I gave him some dry cereal to eat and some milk to drink. Since I didn't know when the refrigeration had failed, I was afraid the milk might not be any good, but I didn't think the unicorn would drink it if it would do him any harm. After he had eaten, he lifted up his head, looked at me and uttered a soft whinny. He put his head under my arm and nuzzled me again; then he tossed it from side to side, whinnying some more. It was clear that he was trying to tell me something. I put my arms around his neck and patted him. "What is it?" I asked gently. "What is it?" I thought perhaps he would be able to communicate with me in that odd, interior way he had used so many hours before, when I had let his mate out of the pen. But he couldn't. Perhaps at that time it had not been he who had spoken to me.

He gave his head another energetic toss and trotted toward the front of the market. I followed. When he came to the window, he stopped and turned. He shook his mane and whinnied yet again. Now I knew what he wanted. He wanted me to follow him out of the building, to go somewhere with him. And it must have something to do with his mate or their foal. He had been seeking help he could trust and had managed to smell me out.

"Wait a minute," I said. He understood me too and remained patiently by the window while I went back to the office and got the rain gear I had hung on a coat-tree in the corner. Putting it over the long johns and flapping shirt I was wearing, I went back to the front of the store. There I used a broom handle to push out the glass that still clung to the edges of the windowframe so that neither the unicorn nor I would cut ourselves as we left. Then I followed him out into the weather.

If I had thought it was raining before, I had been mistaken. That had been a mere passing shower, an opening gambit scarcely worth paying attention to. Now it was raining. It was pouring. The skies had opened, and torrential streams were cascading out of the clouds, innundating the universe.

Somehow, the unicorn and I made our way behind the shopping center. The beast had an uncanny knack for picking out the driest spots and managed to lead me from hillock to hillock as if he were guiding me through a treacherous bog or a sea of quicksand.

It was not long before the little shopping center was lost to my view. I followed the unicorn across flat, empty fields, behind a housing development, past an apartment complex, alongside an empty school. And though we saw all those buildings, we saw no people. It was as if the neighborhood had been depopulated already, though I knew that that could not have happened yet.

Finally we reached a little woods. Here the going was a bit easier for both of us, the leaf and pine needle cover on the ground having enabled it to absorb more water, and the branches of the overhanging trees providing some small protection. A little shed stood alongside the bare remnant of a path. It looked to me like the kind of structure boys might have thrown up for a hideout. It had no floor, and since one side was open, its roof provided little protection in the driving rain. The female unicorn was lying inside, as far from the open side as she could get. This little woods was scarcely sufficient cover for the unicorns—not the kind of place they would have chosen under ordinary circumstances. The female was ill. She had stopped here, or been led here by the male, because she could go no further.

I entered the shed and approached her cautiously. In my hand I held the carton of milk I had carried with me all the way from the supermarket. I put the carton to her mouth, but she was too weak to reach inside and lap at the liquid. So I dipped my fingers in it and held them to her tongue. She licked them weakly, but even that effort was too much for her, and she stopped before she had gotten more than a very little. Her sides were heaving with the effort of breathing, and she had no strength for anything else.

Her nose and tongue were hot and dry. She seemed to be suffering from some kind of fever. I noticed that her teats were engorged and enflamed. When I touched them very gently, they felt hot, and she whimpered with pain. The foal was nowhere to be seen. Though the male had found the female, she had not found her baby, at least not alive, and it was just as well, because she wouldn't have been able to nurse it anyway.

I turned my head and looked at the male. He was staring at me intently, expecting me to do something.

I could think of only one thing, carry her to Jasper. As gently and as carefully as I could, I picked her up in my arms. But how to reach the farm from where we were? Could I find it? I spoke to the male very slowly and clearly, as if I were speaking to a foreigner. "Listen," I said, "I will have to take her back to Jasper. Do you understand that? We will have to try to get back to the farm." Then I added, more to myself than to him, "I doubt that the road I came down is passable now."

Suddenly the unicorn knelt before me. Actually, he wasn't kneeling, but that's what it looked like. His forelegs were stretched out in front of him, his rear legs folded underneath. He wanted me, with his mate in my arms, to climb on his back.

"I can't ride you," I said. "The ground's too soft. With so much weight on you, you'll sink."

He tossed his head and remained in the same position. "Get up," I said. "Lead the way. You know the high ground." But he didn't move. I realized that he wouldn't until I tried it his way. So I climbed on his back. I'd never ridden a horse before, let alone a unicorn. When he rose, my feet hung almost to the sodden earth. He was too small, really, to carry a full-grown woman. Fortunately, I am not a large full-grown woman. I was not uncomfortable.

He trotted off slowly through the copse of trees and out to the open field. Here movement was difficult and he did indeed sink into the mud three or four times. Each time it happened, I slid down his back. He would extricate himself, I would follow him for a few feet, and then, by positioning himself on the ground, he would signal for me to mount him again. He would have it no other way. The female had ceased to moan. Her sides heaved with each painful breath, but her eyes were shut. I think she was unconscious, a mercy in a way.

The unicorn made for the hills, which lay beyond the fields we were crossing. Once we reached them, things were better. The ground was soft, of course, but water had not accumulated here to the same degree it had in the low-lying areas. We came to a narrow gravel road, and moving to the middle of it, he managed to trot along quite smartly. The area was not as heavily developed as the valley, but there were houses here and there along the way. As before, we met no people on foot. A couple of jeeps passed us by, and some pickup trucks, the drivers too intent on the weather to favor us with more than a cursory glance. Maybe afterwards, when they realized what they had seen, they allowed themselves to be amazed; or maybe, through the sheet of rain, they simply took the unicorn for a pony.

I had no idea at first where the unicorn was going. I simply had to trust him. After a while the road forked, and he took the left one, the one that headed downhill. Then I began to sense what he was doing. He was going to come up on the farm from behind, where the ark was kept.

Traveling downhill was much more difficult than moving across the top of the ridge. The unicorn, for all his sure-footedness, stumbled several times, and each time I slid forward. It began to look as if I would surely fall off him, so I pulled his mane until he stopped. Then I got off. "I'll have to walk now," I said. And this time he permitted me to continue on foot.

But we were both exhausted. The female was a dead weight in my arms. The rain was so heavy now that I could scarcely see a foot in front of me. I tripped and fell. It didn't matter. I could not be any muddier or bloodier than I already was. I clutched the unicorn to me tightly as I went down, and her body never touched the ground. But then I didn't want to get up again. I was so tired, so terribly tired. I would have been very happy, I thought, just to lie there in the road and go to sleep, letting my ears, my nose, my mouth, my lungs fill with rain.

But the male was beside me, nuzzling and neighing, so I forced myself to my feet again. From below, I could hear the sound of a vehicle. It came closer, and I saw that it was another jeep. I moved to the side of the extremely narrow road to let it pass. It would have been safer to get off the road entirely, but the ditch that served as the road's shoulder was full of swiftly running water. The unicorn was able to jump it, and he stood behind me, on the water-laden grass, waiting.

But this jeep did not pass us by. It stopped when the driver saw the unicorn and me. He climbed out of his vehicle and walked toward us. It was Sam.

His face was as dark as the heavy, leaden sky above us. But when he saw what I was carrying in my arms, he smiled. "Thank God you found her," he said. "Thank God I found you."

"She's sick," I said.

He nodded. "Get in the jeep," he ordered.

I climbed in the front, next to the driver's seat, still holding the female on my lap. Sam opened the tailgate, and the male leaped in and stretched himself out on the back seat. It seemed to me that he sighed as he laid himself down.

There was no way to turn around. Sam drove a little way further up the hill until he came to a house with a driveway opening out onto the road. There he managed to negotiate a turn and start back down the hill, traveling no more than five miles an hour because the rain hit the windshield as if it were being poured out of the sky in buckets.

I was so glad to be with him again that I was frightened by my own joy. "What are you doing here, Sam?" I scolded. "Why aren't you helping to load the ark?"

"Keep quiet," he replied gruffly. "Can't you see

that I'm having enough trouble driving without trying to answer a lot of silly questions besides?"

I shut up. We crept down the road. And sure enough, in time we came to the back of the farm. The fields were too sodden now for even the jeep to maneuver. So Sam followed the gravel road until it led to the paved one. There he forced the jeep through the water for a few yards until we reached the farm's front drive, where we abandoned the vehicle.

Still carrying the female, I followed Sam and the male into the house. "Wait here," Sam said. "I'll go get Jasper."

No one else was in the house. I lay the unicorn on the couch in the living room. Even Ama would realize that a pretense of normality was no longer possible. It just didn't matter that a muddy animal soiled the pretty flowered chintz slipcover.

I dried the unicorn's pitiful frame with some paper towels I took from the kitchen, and then I covered her with an afghan. She did not seem to regain consciousness. Her breathing grew shallow and ever more labored. The male and I stood beside her, watching helplessly, waiting for Jasper. The male never for a moment took his eyes from her limp, still form.

In time, Sam came back with his older brother. Jasper was carrying the large metal box in which he kept many of his medical supplies. He knelt beside the unicorn and moved his hand gently over her head, neck, flanks and belly. She moaned a little and moved restlessly, but her eyes did not open. Jasper shook his head despairingly. "She's far gone," he said, opening his black box and taking out a hypodermic needle and a vial. He filled the needle and shot the liquid into a vein in the creature's right hind leg.

The unicorn was no grizzly bear. The sharp prick of the needle into a vein no longer protected by a comfortable layer of flesh did what all our painful journeying had not been able to accomplish. It roused her from the unconscious state into which she had fallen. Her eyes flickered open. She turned her head slowly from one of us to the other. First she looked at Sam, and then she looked at me, and then she looked at Jasper. Finally she focused on her mate, and her eyes did not leave him again. She opened her mouth and uttered a faint whinny. Her mate's tongue came out of his mouth and gently he began to lick her white neck. It seemed to me, if such a thing were possible, that she smiled. And then she shut her eyes again.

For another moment the male went on licking her. Then he pulled away. Jasper leaned over and touched her with his wide, strong, stubby-fingered hand. When he straightened up, his face was grim. "She's dead," he said. I could see tears sparkling in his eyes, but he wiped them with the back of his hand. He pressed his lips together before he spoke again. "Come, Sam, Nikki," he said, his voice low and flat. "There's a lot of work to do. Get a rope and bring the male. We'll confine him in a stall in the ark immediately, so he can't get away."

"Oh, come on, Jasper," Sam said, wheeling around to face his brother, "what's the point of that? Why torture the creature any further? Give him some of the phenobarbatol you have there in your box."

Jasper stared at Sam. "I can't do that," he whispered.

"But it ought to be done," Sam replied, his mouth as tight as Jasper's.

"We shouldn't interfere."

"We already have interfered. What would tying him up in the ark be, if not interfering?"

Jasper shook his head slowly. I reached out and put my hand on his arm. "Please, Jasper," I said. "Let's not be any crueler than we have to be."

For a moment Jasper was silent as he looked with anguished eyes from the dead beast's motionless form to the still-living creature at her side. When at last he did speak, his voice was scarcely more than a hoarse croak. "All right," he said. "Do what you want. You'll need twenty cc's of phenobarb. You'll never find a vein. Shoot it into his abdomen." He turned away from us, and with two or three great strides, he was out of the room.

"Can you do it, Sam," I asked, "or should I?"

Sam held out his hand and I held out mine. They were shaking about equally. Sam took mine in his and squeezed it hard, and soon both our hands were still. "You talk to him," he said, "and I'll do it. I think that'll be best. I'm not clever about these things the way Jasper is, but if you keep him still, I think I can do it properly."

I put my arm around the unicorn and kissed him on the brow, as I had that morning when he had awakened me. I kept my arms around him and spoke to him softly. "Goodbye, dear unicorn," I said. "Thank you for everything. I'll never forget you. Do you know that? As long as I live, I'll never forget you."

Awkwardly, Sam plunged the needle into the unicorn's stomach. The animal never flinched. I held him until his body went limp in my arms. His eyes closed, and he sank to the floor. A few minutes later he stopped breathing. He too was dead.

I put my head in my hands and began to sob. Sam put his arm around my shoulders. I lifted up my face and looked into his. His eyes too were full of tears.

"They were different from any other creature on the earth," I said.

"Yes," he agreed. His arms pressed tight around me. "Listen, Nikki," he said. "You asked me a question before."

"Yes," I said. "I wanted to know what you were doing out on the road. But I know what you were doing. You were looking for the unicorns."

"No," he replied, "I was looking for you. If I didn't find you, I wasn't going into the ark."

I sighed, a sigh of relief, a sigh of joy. "I can go with you now," I said. "It's a terrible thing that's happening, an unbearable thing, but I'm not so afraid any more. I want to try to live, since I've been given the chance."

"Thank God," Sam said softly. It was a prayer. "Thank God."

"God has nothing to do with it," I replied sharply. "I still haven't made up my mind about him."

"Listen, my love," Sam said, "God shows Himself in all kinds of ways. This time, a unicorn; next time, who knows what? The important thing is that we know He is with us. In the new world, we must try not to forget that."

"That's up to him, isn't it?"

"Partly," Sam replied. "And partly up to us."

CHAPTER V

OMETIMES AT NIGHT, WHEN I AM wakeful, I think of the unicorns, and my tears begin to fall, unbidden. Sam hears me and he turns and takes me in his arms. His warmth, and the gentle, rocking motion of the ark, sooth me. And then Sam says, "Weep for the unicorns, my love. Weep for the unicorns. For as long as we remember them, they are not wholly gone."